'This spare, urgent debut is not only a polished crime novel, but a hymn to Tokyo and an awkwardly tender love story ... *The Earthquake Bird* is distinguished by its alluring ambiguity'
Lisa Allardice, *Daily Telegraph*

'This is the Japanese novel – obsessive, bordering on the surreal, replete with prosaic details that can be interpreted as clues, but clues to a mystery that remains mysterious' *Observer*

'[Jones] renders Lucy's painful realisation of lost love and missed opportunity with seductive delicacy' Lisa Darnell, *Guardian*

'*The Earthquake Bird* is an astonishingly accomplished debut by Susanna Jones ... It is hard to believe that this skilfully constructed and beautifully written work is a first novel'
Sunday Telegraph

'Gripping and haunting – an unforgettable debut'
Kirkus Reviews

'Fast-paced and claustrophobic ... a subtle portrait of how jealousy blooms from nothing'
The Times

'Susanna Jones is too good to waste her talent faddishly. Literariness and mystery conspire in this debut to produce an engaging narrative' *Spectator*

The Earthquake Bird

Susanna Jones grew up in Yorkshire and studied drama at London University, where she first became fascinated by Japanese culture. She has worked in Japan as a teacher and radio script editor and currently lives in Brighton where she is working on her second novel, which will also be published by Picador. *The Earthquake Bird* was the winner of the CWA John Creasey Memorial Dagger for best first crime novel of 2001.

The Earthquake Bird

SUSANNA JONES

PICADOR

First published 2001 by Picador

This edition published 2002 by Picador
an imprint of Pan Macmillan Ltd
Pan Macmillan, 20 New Wharf Road, London N1 9RR
Basingstoke and Oxford
Associated companies throughout the world
www.panmacmillan.com

ISBN 978-0-330-48502-9

4 5 6 7 8 9

A CIP catalogue record for this book is available
from the British Library.

Phototypeset by Intype London Ltd
Printed and bound in Great Britain by
Mackays of Chatham plc, Chatham, Kent

Visit www.picador.com to read more about all our books and to buy
them. You will also find features, author interviews and news of any author
events, and you can sign up for e-newsletters so that you're always first to hear
about our new releases.

One

Early this morning, several hours before my arrest,
I was woken by an earth tremor. I mention the
incident not to suggest that there was a connection
– that somehow the fault lines in my life came
crashing together in the form of a couple of
policemen – for in Tokyo we have a quake like
this every month or so, sometimes more, and this
morning's was nothing special. I am simply relating
the sequence of events as it happened. It has been
an unusual day and I would hate to forget anything.

I was between the covers of my futon, in a deep
sleep. I awoke to hear my clothes hangers hitting
the sides of the wardrobe. Plates in the kitchen
rattled and the floor creaked. The rocking made
me nauseous but despite that, I hadn't realized why
I was moving. It was only when, from outside, the
familiar sound reached my ears that I understood.

A tinny voice croaked in the wind from far away. I sat up in the dark, shivering.

Since Lily's death and Teiji's disappearance, I have become nervous about many things. I pulled the wardrobe door open and crept beneath the clattering coat hangers. I put on my cycling helmet, reached for the torch that I keep taped to the wall, and crouched in the corner. I shone the light around to check that my whistle and bottle of earthquake water were with me. They were. A cockroach ran across my bare leg and settled on the floor, beside me.

'Go away,' I whispered. 'Get out. Do you hear me? I don't want you here.'

The cockroach's black feelers shifted slightly in my direction. Then it shimmered away and disappeared through an invisible crack in the wall.

It was some moments before I realized that the cupboard was still. The earthquake had stopped. The night was quiet.

I crawled back into the warmth of my futon but couldn't sleep. I knew now I was not alone in my flat. I pulled my pillow under my face and curled up on my side. I have many tricks to deal with the problems of ghosts and insomnia. One of them is to test my Japanese. I took the word for earthquake, *jishin*, and tried to think of words with the same pronunciation but different characters. Putting together *ji*, meaning self, and *shin*, which means trust, produces confidence. With other written characters an earthquake can become an hour hand, a magnetic needle, or be simply oneself, myself. Here I ran out of ideas. There must be more words but I could think of none. I would normally be able to count seven or eight words before dropping off, but this morning my game wasn't working.

I tried another strategy. I imagined Teiji was behind me, circling me with his twiggish arms, rocking me to sleep, as he had done in the happy days when we slept together like spoons. We both loved earthquakes then, as much as we loved thunderstorms and typhoons. I felt comforted by the memory and I may have dozed off for half an hour or so. When I awoke again, the room was light. I folded my futon and kicked it into the cupboard. I grabbed a packet of instant noodles for my lunch and drank a quick cup of tea. At seven o'clock, I set off for work feeling no more tired, no worse than I have felt for the last few weeks. I expected a normal day at my office.

*

The police came for me in the afternoon. I was at my desk working on a translation of a new design of bicycle pump. I was concentrating hard and didn't notice the arrival of my visitors. The work was not particularly difficult – my job is to translate tedious technical documents and I do it very well – but it took my mind off recent, disastrous events. I became aware that my colleagues had stopped working and were looking in the direction of the door. I raised my head. Two policemen stood in the entrance. I wasn't surprised. I'm sure no one was. My co-workers looked from the police to me and back again.

To be arrested in the middle of the office, in front of an unsupportive audience, was a degradation I didn't want. I leapt from my seat hoping to pre-empt the police officers' strike.

'It's for me,' I muttered. 'I think they just want to ask some more questions. No big deal.'

And before I could cross the room, 'Ms Fly? We're taking you to the police station for questioning in connection with the disappearance of Lily Bridges. Bring your alien registration card.'

I stood before the two dark blue uniforms and tried to edge them toward the door.

'It's in my pocket. I never go anywhere without

it. But I've already answered a lot of questions. I can't imagine I have anything else to tell you.'

'There are new developments. We'd like you to come with us down to the car.'

I was nervous. There was only one potential development that I could think of, but I didn't dare ask my question. Had they found the missing parts of Lily's body? By now the disparate pieces may have been washed ashore with the tide, or caught in nets by the night fishermen. Perhaps the police had been able to put her back together again and make an official identification. That would be a formality. According to the newspapers, the police knew they'd found Lily.

Nothing has been the same in the office since that morning a couple of weeks ago when someone brought in the *Daily Yomiuri* and passed it quietly from desk to desk until, by the afternoon, it had reached mine. The headline announced: 'Woman's torso recovered from Tokyo Bay. Believed to be missing British bartender Lily Bridges.'

And no one would look at me after that, not properly. I don't know whether they thought I was a murderer or whether the whole horror of Lily's death had left them too embarrassed to talk to me.

The police led me out of the room – as if I didn't

know the way – and down to the car on the street. I didn't look up. I knew my colleagues were watching from the window but there was no need to wave them goodbye. I shouldn't think we'll meet again. I shall miss one of them, my friend, Natsuko. She wanted to believe in me, but the headline was too much even for her and she has deserted me.

My own reaction to the news story was that Lily wouldn't have approved of the wording, brief though it was. She was a bartender only in Japan. At home in Hull she had been a nurse. She was a fine nurse, as I discovered on our hike in Yaman-ashi-ken, when I slipped and fell on the moun-tainside. She led me down and bandaged my ankle with such efficient compassion that I almost cried. But in the bar she was clumsy and meek. Her voice was so high and whiny it made people want to jump behind the bar and get their own drinks. The bar job was only intended to be temporary.

But now Lily's dead and I'm in a police station. It is my first brush with the Japanese legal system, apart from a few avuncular questions when Lily first disappeared. I'm not sure what they want from me this time, but it seems serious. I am sitting on a bench in a corridor. The men who brought me here have gone away and there are two policemen fussing around nearby. An old fat one and a young thin one. The fat one is persuading the thin one to speak English to me to find out whether or not I can speak Japanese. I have not bothered to tell them that my Japanese is fluent, that indeed I am a professional translator. It is a fact they should know, if they know anything at all. They have reached an agreement. The thin one faces me.

'Hello. I'm going to be the interpreter.' His English is slow, hesitant.

'Hello.'

'Could you please tell me your full name?'

'It's on my alien registration card. I gave it to someone before.'

This information is imparted to the other officer, in Japanese. The reply comes back in Japanese, then English.

'It's not my job to know what happened to your alien registration card. Your full name.'

'Lucy Fly.'

The fat one knits his brow.

'Rooshy Furai,' I say, making an effort to be cooperative. When the police questioned me before, my friend Bob warned that I should try to act normal, although it goes against my nature, and I will be as obliging as I can.

'I'm thirty-four years old.'

He doesn't respond

'I was born in the year of the snake, in fact.'

'And you work in Tokyo, in Shibuya,' the old, fat policeman says in Japanese. When it's relayed into English, I reply, 'That's right.'

'Company name?'

Again, I wait for the translation before I answer, 'Sasagawa.'

'You're an editor there?'

My young, thin friend obediently conveys this to me.

'A translator. Japanese to English.' I expect the coin to drop but it doesn't.

'How long have you worked there?'

'About four years.'

'So you speak Japanese.'

The interpreter says, 'So you speak Japanese.'

'Yes,' I say. *Wake up*, I think.

'Yes, she does.'

The policeman looks at me. It is a suspicious, unfriendly look that I feel I have not deserved. Not yet.

'*Pera pera*,' I say. *Fluently.*

'You didn't say so.'

'I wasn't asked.'

The interpreter leaves, in something of a huff. I am glad to be rid of him. I didn't think much of his accent. I'm left with the old, fat man.

My captor shows me to a chair in a small room. He sits opposite me and looks everywhere but at my face. I'm not complaining. Why should he have to look at my face? Lucy is not an oil painting, as everyone who has seen her knows. When I am comfortably seated, though, he forces his eyes upon my face only to find that now he can't let go. There's something about my eyes, I know this.

'I want you to tell me about the night Lily Bridges-san disappeared.'

'Do we know which night she disappeared?'

'The night after which she was never seen again. As far as we know, you were the last person she spoke to.'

'I've already told you about that.'

'I'd like you to tell me again.'

'I was in my flat. The doorbell rang. I answered it. It was Lily. We spoke for a minute or so and she left.'

'And?'

'I went back inside.'

'After that?'

'Nothing. I don't remember. I was bringing my washing in when Lily called. I probably returned to doing that.'

'One of your neighbours saw you on the walkway outside your front door, speaking to Bridgessan.'

I rolled my eyes. 'Then presumably he or she saw what I just told you.'

He stares at me. Like a teacher waiting patiently for a child's confession, knowing it will come.

'OK. I went after her about five minutes later. There was something I'd forgotten to tell her.'

'So you spoke to her again?'

'No, I didn't find her.'

'You assumed she was going to the station?'

'Yes. I don't know where else she could have gone. I don't believe she knew my area of Tokyo well.'

'The route from your apartment to the station is fairly straightforward, is it not? And the streets are well lit at night.'

'That's true, but I didn't find her. I don't know where she went.'

'Would you tell me the nature of the conversation you had at your front door?'

I shake my head.

'You don't remember it?'

'I remember it.'

'Then please share it with me.'

'No.'

'Your neighbour reported that you were angry. You shouted at Bridges-san.'

'I don't shout.'

'You weren't angry?'

'I was angry.'

'Your neighbour said that you appeared to be carrying something, a bundle of some kind.'

I snort. 'Who is this neighbour? Miss Marple?'

I know very well that it was my vacuuming neighbour from next door. She has always struck me as having a fertile imagination. She vacuums aggressively for hours every day and sometimes in the middle of the night. There must be some wild ideas inside her head. Besides, she is my only immediate neighbour. There are just two flats above the petrol station and one is mine. I suppose it's a pity we never became friends, but it's too late now.

His face is blank.

'I was carrying nothing. Nothing at all.'

He stares at me. 'Think carefully. Please.'

I think hard, to be polite, but I am feeling tired.

'As I told you, I was bringing my washing in. It's possible that when I answered the door, I was holding some item of clothing. But still, I am not so absent-minded that I could have gone after Lily with something in my hands. And if I had found myself running down the street with a pair of knickers in my grasp, I would remember.'

'I wonder what it could be that your neighbour saw.'

'My hands were empty.'

'Bridges-san was a close friend of yours.'

I pause. 'Yes.'

'Tell me about your friendship.'

'No.'

'Lily was your best friend, wasn't she?'

'She became a close friend. I didn't know her very long.'

'Other friends?'

'Mine or hers?'

'Yours.'

I am not going to tell him of Teiji, my friend above all friends.

'Natsuko. She's my colleague. Bob. He's American. I met him in the dentist's waiting room. I taught him how to say "a dull nagging pain" in

Japanese. He's an English teacher so he can't really speak Japanese. And Mrs Yamamoto. She ran the string quartet I used to play in. Mrs Ide and Mrs Katoh too. Second violin and viola.'

'Did Lily Bridges know these people?'

'Only Natsuko and Bob. Mrs Yamamoto died before Lily came to Japan. She never met Mrs Ide and Mrs Katoh.'

'Why did Lily Bridges come to Japan? What is your understanding of her intentions?'

'She liked *Hello Kitty.*'

He looks up, suspicious.

'I don't know why she came.'

I do know. I'm not going to tell him about Andy, her boyfriend, and how he followed her and planted bugging devices in her handbag and beat up the window cleaner for climbing up his ladder to the bedroom window while Lily was changing her top, as if he could have known she was there. I will not tell him that she came to Japan secretly, giving up a job she loved, to escape from that boyfriend. I won't tell him because he already knows. I told the police before. So did Bob.

He stands and opens the door to let another one in. Now there are two. I squint to read the kanji on their name badges. The old one is called Kameyama (turtle mountain) and the new one is Oguchi (small mouth). Oguchi is young, with soft, hairless arms and the stoop of a teenager who has grown too quickly. He sits a little further back than Kameyama and looks worried. Kameyama leaves the room saying that he will be back soon. Oguchi plays with the left knee of his trousers. His fingers are long and bony, like his nose which he reaches to scratch. His eyes dart all around the cell but he knows I'm watching him and he doesn't look at me. He bats a mosquito from his neck. It dances up before his eyes and moves closer and closer to his face. He attempts bravely to ignore it but it is starting to make a fool of him. Then, with more violence than is necessary, he smashes his hands together, wipes the squelch nonchalantly on a white handkerchief. He turns his eyes to the door, waiting hopefully for Kameyama's return. I notice he is blushing slightly. I think he fancies me.

Kameyama is very busy wherever he is and does not reappear for a while. Oguchi bows his head and scribbles something on a notepad. I am left to wonder at my future, and what control I now have. I think of Teiji and how, if he were here with me, I would not care what happened next. But it's nicer to reflect on the past, and more useful. If I think of what has already happened, I can start to make out how the past became the present, how my friendships turned to nothing, and why I'm here.

I picture Teiji sitting opposite me in Oguchi's chair, taking my hand and stroking the tips of my fingers, caressing them like soft cool water. I shiver at the imagined sensation and that is enough to take me back to Shinjuku, the place where I first saw him. That night I believed he was made of rain and nothing else.

I was wandering around central Tokyo. It was soon after Mrs Yamamoto's string quartet had disbanded and I was now at a loss every Sunday evening. I came to the famous skyscrapers of Nishi-Shinjuku and had every intention of walking straight past. Guidebook writers are enthralled by this *Blade Runner* setting of futuristic buildings, but to Lucy's mind they are nothing more than dull hotels, banks, and government offices that happen to be very high and cast long shadows. Exciting if you're standing on the fifty-second floor, a crick in the neck if you're on the pavement. It was raining steadily and I was the only person not bothering to use an umbrella. Umbrellas are cumbersome and a menace to the streets with their inhuman span and sharp, dangerous spokes. Lucy's skin is waterproof and her clothes can always be dried.

A young man stood in front of the Keio Plaza Hotel, with streams of umbrella-wielding people passing him on both sides. He was leaning over a puddle, apparently taking photographs of it. Water slid over his hair and face but he seemed not to notice. His camera clicked and he moved fluidly to the other side of the puddle. I stared. He appeared to be made of water and ice. I had never seen a man with such delicate fingers, sharp brittle shoulder-blades, transparent brown eyes. He glinted in the neon dark more sharply than the vast ice sculptures of the Sapporo Festival I had marvelled at when I first came to Japan. He was an exhibit of the Tokyo night and so beautiful that I couldn't walk past him.

I went to his puddle and looked in to see what had captivated him. The reflection of the Keio Plaza Hotel divided the dirty water into two. On one side were shiny windows and lights, on the other, darkness and a couple of cigarette butts floating. To my eyes the stubby ends looked like people jumping from the hotel windows, but he was looking deeper into the puddle than I could see. I took a small step forward so that the tips of my shoes entered the water and were reflected over the hotel. He didn't look up. He shifted round the puddle with the camera against his eye all the time. Then he shot the picture, including my feet. I kept my position and he lifted his head to look at me. His eyes searched my face as if he couldn't quite find what he wanted. He put his camera back to his eye and looked at me through the viewfinder, like a child peering through an empty toilet roll tube to see the world in another way. And the camera clicked and flashed. Those were the first pictures he took of me. I have never seen them.

The moment was so intimate that I knew it must be followed by an even deeper intimacy. After all, I had flirtatiously invited myself into his photograph. He had led me in and captured me with a single snap. My feet and face were now inside his camera. He had got me inside him and the next step was obvious, though brazen.

We may have spoken, but if we did, I don't remember it. I don't even remember the point at which I knew where we were going. I believe that we walked together in silence. We could hardly afford a room at the Keio Plaza – no one can – and so we headed to his apartment in Shin-Okubo.

It is a walk of about twenty minutes but another part of Tokyo altogether. We left the neon towers and entered backstreet Tokyo. Old houses nestled between small apartment buildings. Narrow grey streets were lined with tiny shops and bars. Orange lanterns decorated cheap eating houses. Alley cats hissed at dogs that barked from balconies. We passed many puddles but he took no more photographs until we reached his apartment.

I can hear the click of his key in the door. Then, in lamplight and with the curtains open, he took one final picture. It was of my naked body. I was kneeling on the bed, leaning back, waiting to become beautiful under his touch. I didn't mind being looked at through the camera. It had more kindness than a naked eye. A camera can't blink or sneer, at least not when the picture is taken. It saves its opinion until the film is developed.

And then Teiji closed his eyes. He did not open them again until much later and I like to believe it was because the image of my body was framed under each eyelid. He was watching that still image when I crawled on top of his ice body, rocked him back and forth until the ice turned to water and his icicle penis melted inside me. I stayed in my position long after our breathing had slowed, wondering how this had happened so easily. Then I lifted myself off his slender frame, pink and aching inside and outside with something that felt unusually close to joy.

Since his eyes were closed and the room was light, I took the opportunity to look around the space to acquaint myself better with this man. The room was like a large cupboard. His clothes hung from the walls, blue and grey jumpers, soft T-shirts, old trousers and a pair of jeans. There was a tie hanging over the curtain rail but it was covered in dust and I could see no shirt that it could be worn with. There was no bookcase, just piles of books stacked high. I could not see the titles. On top of the books were piles of CDs. There was a large begonia in the corner of the room with a pair of swimming goggles entwined among the leaves. There were three or four cameras strewn on the floor, two cardboard boxes full of camera shop envelopes. But there were no photographs on display anywhere. The walls were painted white, a little dirty. Apart from his clothes they were bare. The curtains twitched against them in the night breeze, bluish white.

We must have slept, but I don't remember. In the morning, he took me to the small noodle restaurant where he worked. I learned later that it belonged to his uncle and he would inherit it one day. It wasn't open yet but we sat behind the scratched wooden counter at the back of the shop and drank tall glasses of iced barley tea. A small fan on the wall behind turned noisily from side to side, blowing cold air down the back of my neck. We didn't look at each other. Our bodies touched, side by side, and I absorbed his warmth, made it mine.

Oguchi is watching me now. He pours me a glass of water and I am grateful for this apparent token of kindness, though for all I know it is a right written into the Japanese constitution. I am hot. I dip my fingers into the glass, smear cold water across my face. He seems to take this as a sign that the ice is broken.

'You have been in Japan a long time. Nine years?'

Is this part of the official questioning or is he chatting me up? I'm not certain. Surely he should be recording everything I say, to be used in evidence against me.

'Ten.'

'What brought you here?'

This is more like it. I have been asked this question fifty thousand times in ten years. I don't have an honest answer because there isn't one, or I am not honest enough to think of it. But I have a few pat answers for when I'm asked. This is a special occasion and so I use all of them.

'An interest in Japanese culture, I wanted to study the language, I needed to save some money, I wanted to see the world, I wanted to get away from dreary old England, I like tofu.' I am enjoying this so I ad lib and give him a few more. 'Chopsticks are lighter than knives and forks and are held in the same hand – you don't get that metallic taste, the trains are so much better here, both reasonably priced and reliable, sumo wrestlers have beautiful calves although their thighs can be too dimply for my liking. It's so clever the way you can pay your bills at a convenience store instead of having to wait until the banks are open and then being late for work. The irises are beautiful in May, just as good as the puffy pink cherry blossoms that people go on and on about like they do with geisha who are not so special when you look at them close up because you can see their spots even through all that make-up, schoolgirls on the trains are always laughing, I can't stand my family.'

I can see he is not sure where to take this. I am a little surprised, and rather impressed, by my fluent collection. I'll be quiet now. I will not tell Oguchi anything more than he asks for, because everything else I say will lead to Lily. I will have a job convincing the police that I am innocent, but one thing is indisputable. If Lily had never met me, she would be alive now.

The facts of Lily's death, as far as I know at this stage in the interview, are few and easily open to misinterpretation. She had been in Tokyo for several months when one night she disappeared. A few days later the torso of a young woman was fished out of Tokyo Bay, with a couple of unattached but matching limbs, I forget which ones. Although the police were unable to make an official identification because there were no hands and so no fingerprints, it seemed to be widely accepted that the body was Lily's. As you know, my connection with the event was that she had been seen knocking on the door of my apartment earlier in the evening of her disappearance. My neighbour saw the door open, spotted me in the doorway speaking angrily to Lily, and saw Lily walking away. Then she watched as I followed a few minutes later, *carrying a bundle*. That is certainly a lie. Why didn't she say that she saw me tuck a revolver into my shirt after closing the front door? Or that I held a dagger before me as I walked? I have never denied the other facts though I have chosen not to detail the conversation we had at that time.

One of the suspects was Lily's ex-boyfriend, though unless he was using a fake passport and travelling very quickly, it seems that he was back in England with a fool-proof alibi, worse luck for me. On the day in question he was captured on closed-circuit television, entering a chip shop in Goole and asking for cod and chips with a pickled egg for lunch. He fiddled with the hem of his anorak and scratched his ear before reaching into the pocket of his jeans for a couple of pound coins. The other main suspect is the usual Mr X who shows up in dark alleyways at night in every country in the world to remind us, by what he does to a woman's body, that the definition of a human being includes that which is not human.

Without further evidence it is hard to imagine what progress the police could have made. I don't suppose my friend is going to tell me, until I give him something more about Lily. I remain silent; my thoughts return to Teiji.

The morning after our first encounter I awoke early, scribbled my address on a scrap of paper and left it under his camera before we went to the noodle shop. I didn't write my telephone number. I wanted him to come and find me.

The doorbell rang while I was in the shower. A week had passed since our first meeting. I could tell from the sound of the bell – less sudden than usual, a quietly confident ring – that it was Teiji's soft fingertip pushing the button, so I didn't bother to pick up a towel. I opened the door more narrowly than usual – even then I knew my neighbour was nosy – and let Teiji slip through.

If only I could remember what he said to me. He might have told me I was beautiful, for I'm sure that he did say so sometimes. He may have exclaimed upon finding me so perfectly, nakedly prepared for him. Perhaps I don't remember what he said that day because perhaps he said nothing. It may have been that we went straight into my room where we fell immediately into lovemaking. And afterwards, with a sheet around me, I looked into his camera while it snapped up my image. We could have done all this without a single word. And yet, if he never spoke, how did I even know that his name was Teiji?

But every time I remember Teiji what I am doing is *not* remembering Lily. It's all wrong. I still have not introduced Lily, not properly. I have been putting it off, hoping she would walk in of her own accord. But I was wrong. She is already here, you see. She is there in the shadows of the cell's corners, in the buzzing of the light over my head, the fruit fly at the corner of my vision that may just be a speck in my eye. When I lean forward my hair flops over my left temple and then I know Lily is inside my face. Sometimes I feel I am walking not quite like myself – my steps are shorter, quicker, a scuttle, almost – and so I know she's got into my legs too.

I blink and realize that Kameyama has returned and together he and Oguchi are staring at me.

'You can't just sit and gaze into space. You will have to tell me about Bridges-san. It won't do to sit here all night and not tell me anything. You knew her well. We already know that.'

'Yes, I did.' But not well enough. That is all.

Kameyama shouts questions at me, one after another. I close my eyes and ears. I see and hear nothing.

Two

I met Lily in a bar in Shibuya. It was only a few months ago, though it seems longer. She was with Bob, the teacher I'd become acquainted with in a dentist's waiting room, and some other English teachers, and I did not want to be there. I rarely socialized with other foreigners, and since I'd started seeing Teiji I had no desire or need to see anyone else. But Bob had called to ask me especially.

'There's a new woman working at the British bar I go to, Lucy. Well, girl really. She's a bag of nerves. She's never been abroad before and she looks as if she's just landed on the moon. I don't know how she's going to cope.'

'Oh.' What was it to me?

'She needs help. I mean, she needs to find a flat. She's living in a seedy gaijin house now with some real assholes and she's the only woman. If she doesn't get out soon, I think she'll crack up.'

'It's not hard to find a flat. I've done it.'

'Lily doesn't speak a word of Japanese.'

An unusual name. I liked it. 'So can't you help her?'

'I thought you'd be able to help. You found your place on your own so you know what's around and what to look for. Besides, your Japanese is better than anyone else's. It was just an idea.'

'It sounds more like a plan than an idea.' But I am a Leo and respond well to flattery. Bob had won my help.

'Will you come out for a drink with us on Friday? We're going to an izakaya in Shibuya. Just meet her, yeah? If you don't want to go round estate agents with her, at least you could give her some advice.'

It's not that I'm so ungenerous as a rule but I wanted to spend every minute of my time with Teiji, or by myself, thinking about Teiji. There was no space for this wimpish woman. Lily. I imagined a tall, beautiful woman with pale skin and a long white neck. She'd be in a corner of the bar sipping gin and tonic from an elegant glass. She would look at me and smile serenely. Beautiful women are always pleased to look at me. My dark eyes are too piercing to be beautiful. I am the ugliness that defines their beauty. For that matter, men are pleased to look at me too. They think, I may not get a supermodel, but at least I know I can do better than get her. You could say, then, that I have a unique beauty; people like to look at my face, they like me to be around for aesthetic reasons. I envied Lily before I'd seen her.

I entered the bar and found the English teachers sitting in a corner, talking loudly about work. Lily was the only one of the group I didn't know. She did have pale skin but she was short and jagged, all elbows and knees. She had a large tuft of dyed auburn hair that rose an inch or so from her head and then flopped over her left eye. Her eyes were dark, like mine, but without expression. They sat beneath her eyebrows like two fat plums. She peered at me from under the tuft. Her eyes and fingers twitched. She was attractive, but also slightly comical and instead of envying her, I found myself smiling.

"Ello."

I located her accent immediately, to East Yorkshire. I am no Professor Higgins, it just happens that she sounded exactly like the girls I was at school with. Years of travelling, speaking other languages and trying to disassociate myself from my origins have left me with no traces of my original accent. I speak in a neutral, hard-to-locate voice, and it suits me very well. I have no patience with people who carry their accent like a flag or anthem, determined to assault you with their provincial jingoism.

Lily smiled at me, then twitched and fiddled with her fringe.

'I like this Japanese beer,' she said to me. 'It's great.'

'I'll have Guinness. When did you arrive?'

'Here? The pub?'

'No. Japan.'

'Oh.' She dropped cigarette ash on her lap and brushed it clumsily with her fingers. Her hands were shaking slightly. 'Last Friday. To be honest I never thought I'd get here and now that I am I'm not really sure why, you know.'

I nodded.

'It's like, I've got to get used to a new home, a new language, everything. I don't know how I'm going to do it, you know, everybody else really seems to fit in. This is my first night off and I'm all at sea.'

'You've only just got here. Of course it's hard at first. What brought you to Japan?'

'I was in a relationship that ended. My boyfriend, Andy, I left him, you see.'

I thought she was about to start crying. She flicked her tuft off her face and lowered her voice, as if to let me in on a secret.

'Well, I had to. We were going to get married but it all went horrible. And I was in a terrible state and I decided I just had to leave, you know. You see, he was very possessive and even though I don't think he liked me very much, he still followed me round sometimes, to make sure I didn't have fun with anyone else. I really don't know what he thought I was doing. So I wanted to escape from him, but it wasn't just that. I wanted to start things all over again so I thought I'd travel, you know, see the world and that.'

'Good,' I said. 'A new start. I hear you're looking for somewhere to live.'

'Yeah. The place I'm living now, it's . . .'

She appeared to run out of steam and sat staring at the table. I knew the kind of place it was and I knew its inhabitants. I've seen them. A run-down building with a bunch of Western men coming home nightly with their conquests. Men who would be nothing special in their home countries suddenly find themselves sought after by women because of their race. They get the pretty women they've never had before and they have moved up to the next link in the food chain. It goes to their heads. They live in splendid semen-saturated squalor. As many women as possible, as often as possible and a fresh lie to each of them. And there are cockroaches too.

'I've just got to get out. Can you help me? I don't speak any Japanese and I really don't know how to go about this. I only came to Japan because my friend knew about this job at a bar here. Excuse me, I must go to the loo.'

She darted out of the room. I turned to Bob.

'I've got nothing in common with her. I don't want to get stuck with looking after her.'

'Lucy, she's new here.'

'Tokyo's full of foreigners who are new here. Every day more arrive. If I looked after all of them, I'd never have a life of my own.'

'All right, all right. I just got the impression that she's lonely.'

'Everybody's lonely.'

'Fine.'

I thought of my first Japanese friend, Natsuko,

and her smiling face welcoming me when I arrived, knowing nothing, in Tokyo.

'Bob, I'll help her find a flat, but I'm not getting stuck with her.' I hissed, 'I can't stand East Yorkshire people.'

'I didn't know you were so prejudiced.' He laughed. 'Besides, I thought Yorkshire was your part of the world.'

'It is. That's my point.'

Lily returned.

'I'll take you to find a flat. It's not so hard but there are places that will rent to foreigners and ones that won't. Also, money's complicated. As well as a deposit and rent in advance, you'll probably have to pay key money – like a deposit except that you'll never see it again.'

'I don't care. I've brought my savings.'

'You'll care when you see how much it is. And you'll have to have a Japanese guarantor.'

'My boss'll do that. He said so.'

'That's fine, then. I'll translate for you, if you want.'

'Thanks very much. It's all a bit different from Hull.'

'It certainly is.'

Lily caught something in my voice. 'Where are you from?'

'Near Hull, the coast.'

'What a coincidence! Me too. Fancy running into someone from home all the way out here. That's made me feel a lot better, that has. It's so good to have friends from home, don't you think so?'

'I haven't lived there for a very long time.'

'It's your roots that count.'

'Plants and trees have roots. People have legs.'

We arranged to meet the following weekend. I thought that I would help her find her flat and never see her again.

That was the beginning of Lily, in my story. Clumsy and faltering. It was not so much of an entrance after all but then, as you will see, Lily was so much better at exits.

I am not sharing this information with the policemen, not unless things get nasty. For the moment I am ignoring them quite successfully. Kameyama is still shouting at me. His voice fades in and out of my hearing. I catch fragments. He tells me that if I don't cooperate they will keep me here all night, bring a colleague or two to ask more questions. He suggests we all sit quietly while I think about what happened, and what I can tell them. The consequences of my words and my silences will be severe. He doesn't need to remind me that Japan maintains the use of the death penalty – hanging, in fact – for certain murders. He informs me, unnecessarily, that I am unlikely to get much sleep tonight.

And silence falls in this small room with its table and three chairs. The room is a cliché but I want to believe my feelings are wholly original. For what Lucy desires now, more than anything in this world, is a bowl of noodles. Specifically she would like udon, big fat white worms of noodles, but she would settle for squiggly ramen, or even delicate skinny soba. She would like noodles in a big brown bowl, with a raw egg broken into the soup and a pair of lacquer chopsticks with which to catch them and gobble them up. I bend my head toward my imaginary bowl, as if to inhale the flavour.

The only way to eat noodles is, of course, to fish them out of the broth, partially, and suck them straight into your mouth, slurping continuously until the bowl has nothing left but soup and a few floating morsels. Most Westerners who come to

Japan find it hard to do. If you have been brought up with the guilt of noisy mastication, it is impossible to slurp well. And if you can't slurp, you can't suck the noodles into your mouth so it becomes impossible to eat them efficiently. Most people give up halfway through the bowl or eat horribly slowly. I took to slurping immediately. When I discovered that Teiji worked in a noodle shop, I knew he was mine. Was it a coincidence that he worked in such a place?

Yesterday, I went back to the noodle shop. I knew that I was moving further away from Lily and Teiji with each hour that passed, and so I returned, ludicrously hoping that I would see Teiji. I wasn't going to speak to him. I just wanted to catch a distant glimpse of his shoulder-blades under his T-shirt, or his profile as he wiped the tables. But I knew perfectly well that the shop had changed hands and Teiji would have no reason to be there. I knew that but, as any good stalker will appreciate, it did not stop me looking.

I could see from the outside that the shop had changed. It was cleaner, brighter, and there was a new name over the door. The grime had gone from the windows and the slanting doorstep had been levelled out.

I went inside and sat nervously at a counter that ran along the back wall of the shop. A young, fresh waiter took my order for tamago udon. While I waited I mopped my forehead with my hand towel. I took a pair of wooden chopsticks and snapped them apart. The steaming bowl arrived and I began to eat. The noodles were delicious but, perhaps because of the nature of recent events, when I looked into the bowl I found myself thinking of a murder case I'd read about here a few years ago.

The killer had a street stand selling noodles. He also had a dead body to dispose of. In order to avoid the fingerprint problem he had hacked off the corpse's hands. He then proceeded to boil the outer layers of skin off the hands by dropping them into the hot noodle broth, on the street, under the unknowing eyes of his hungry customers. I don't know how he was caught but I wondered about it. Did a passer-by notice, out of the corner of her eye, a human hand floating to the surface of the delicious bubbling soup? Did a customer find that the noodles tasted a little gamier than they should?

I thought of Lily and my noodles tasted sweeter for a few seconds. Then I sensed Teiji behind me, watching and frowning upon my act of metaphysical cannibalism. I dropped my chopsticks. One of them fell and hit the floor. I bent to reach it, feeling tears accumulating, and knocked the bowl off the counter. It smashed and the noodles and soup splashed across the tiles. I felt the eyes of everyone in the restaurant studiously avoiding my direction. Perhaps in Britain I would have had a round of applause. I tried to call for a waiter but my voice was taken up with quiet, deep sobs that sounded as if they were coming from someone else.

A waiter rushed toward me with a dustpan, brush and mop. He told me that there was no problem though I could see he hardly knew which implement to use first. Before I could say no thank you, another waiter had slipped a full bowl of noodles onto the counter in front of me, compliments of the shop. I had no choice but to start again. After a few minutes my childish crying came to a stop. I dried my eyes and nose with my hand towel and, feeling a little better, began to eat.

By the time the last inch of noodle was inside me, my eyes were only slightly sore. I felt as if I had been bandaged up. By whom? By the noodles, though I caught myself thinking of a kind nurse in my childhood, and then of the other nurse I knew, Lily. I left the shop feeling fed and satisfied.

I will try to sustain myself now on the memory

of the taste. My back is beginning to ache from sitting in this uncomfortable chair. I suppose I am allowed to stand for a moment and stretch. I move, and feel a little better. The policemen stare at me with identical expressions of weariness. I ignore them.

As I have said, I agreed to meet Lily and help her find a home. So, though I had no interest in her at all, I waited for her at the station in Itabashi. She was ten minutes late and apologized about it for the next fifteen. She rabbited on about the awfulness of her current accommodation and expected me to listen. I paid attention to some of it but not all. I find it hard to concentrate for long in conversation and my mind wandered to other things. I started to think about the first time I tried to rent an apartment in Tokyo and was turned down by streetfuls of estate agents because I was foreign. It took weeks to find a place. In the end I settled for a poky room above a noisy garage because I was tired of hunting. I have come to love that room, though, and had hoped I would never have to move. These days it is easier for foreigners and easier still for Lily because she had me to help her.

She rattled on.

'Andy wanted to get married and I did too but I didn't want to hurry and I thought we should wait till we had more money saved up. He thought that meant I was seeing someone else and I was just trying to put off the wedding so he got more and more jealous. I mean, jealous of a man who didn't exist! It got to be embarrassing because he'd start to suspect people, you know, like the milkman and that. He had a go at one of his friends once for saying hello to me in the street and that was too much so I left him and went to stay with a friend. Anyway, he guessed where I was so I moved to her sister's and then another friend's and finally someone told me I could get work here, and I did. Sorry, am I really boring you with all this?'

'Not at all.' I was not answering to be polite but because it was true. I wasn't bored because I wasn't listening to much of it. I was somewhere in my own thoughts while her words covered the air around us like wallpaper. I paid just enough attention to have a grasp of the topic for future reference.

'What about you?' She turned her head to me. 'Have you got a boyfriend?'

I couldn't demean Teiji by referring to him with

such a common and banal term. On the other
hand, I supposed he was my boyfriend. We didn't
exactly date but I couldn't say he wasn't my boyfriend. Lover, perhaps. But what was I to him?
I didn't know and for some reason I didn't feel
comfortable thinking about it.

'Mm,' I said quickly and changed the subject.
'There are several estate agents along here.'

I suggested Lily find a flat near a station, on a
high floor. Even in Japan a woman living alone
can't be too careful. But Lily wanted to be somewhere quiet, away from stations, and on the
ground floor because it would feel more like a
house and not a flat.

'It'll be a bit cheaper then,' I conceded.

One-roomed flats in Tokyo are pretty much like
each other. All the places we looked at had polished wooden floors, were six tatami mats in size.
The kitchens were small but clean and new. They
had narrow balconies and unit bathrooms, a big
plastic bubble of a room where each facility is part
of the mould. Some flats were older than others,
some noisier. I enjoyed looking. Lucy cannot visit
a home, occupied or not, without imagining herself
into it.

One had a balcony that overlooked a crooked old house with flowerpots on the garage roof and several cats asleep among them. I thought it might be possible to climb down to the roof without the residents of the house noticing. It would be a good place to sit and read on a warm afternoon.

The next flat was so dark that even with all the lights on there was just an eerie yellow dinge. The balcony was faced by a dirty grey apartment building. When I looked down from the balcony I could see through the windows into the rooms. I spied on a kitchen.

A middle-aged man was putting a pan on the stove. He lit the gas, stood and stared at it. A woman – his wife, I guessed – came and stood with her back to him, fiddled around in a cupboard. It looked as if neither knew the other was there but the room was so small they must have known. The woman left the kitchen and I went back into the flat where Lily was now inspecting the bathroom. She had her tongue out in concentration, like a child painting a picture.

'What do you think?' I asked.

'The place is a goldfish bowl and there's no natural light. Let's go.'

It was the right answer for Lily. Had it been my

choice I would have taken it. Lucy could imagine crouching on her balcony at night, peering from behind a drying towel into the lives of her neighbours. From the windows of my own flat that is impossible. The petrol station beneath my balcony provides me with day-long entertainment, but at night it's quiet. I would have liked to be able to see into a kitchen or living room.

Finally Lily chose a place that had big wide windows and a small park outside. Its only drawback was that it was old and so more vulnerable in an earthquake.

'Bob said there haven't been any tremors for ages,' Lily said.

'But that's when you have to worry. When you have a series of small ones it means that everything's OK. If there's nothing for a long time then you know that the big one could hit.'

'I didn't know that.'

We went to the estate agent's and I helped Lily sign documents. I was tired and ready to go home but Lily was intent on thanking me.

'Let me at least buy you a cuppa somewhere. Go on.'

I didn't want to be with her. I didn't dislike her and yet I saw her as a representative of the place of my childhood. I couldn't like her. I knew that if we spent more time together she would start to talk about Yorkshire again and its godforsaken beauties and comforts.

'I really am tired. You go. One of the nice things about Japan is that it's perfectly OK to be in a cafe or restaurant alone. No one will pester you or stare at you.'

'I don't even know how to order a cup of coffee. I don't know any Japanese at all. Sure you won't come with me?'

Her blank eyes flickered suddenly with fear.

'I'll come, then. Just to show you how to order in a cafe.'

We found a small, ferociously air-conditioned coffee shop. Lily sat and put her bag on the floor beside her. It was a refreshing sight. I had forgotten that people put bags on floors in Britain. In Japan the floor is considered too dirty. I rarely carry a bag. I like to stuff the things I need into my pockets, so it is not an issue that touches me. A handbag is part of a femininity I have never felt I had the right to aspire to. Still, I liked to see Lily put her bag on the floor.

When the waitress came, Lily whispered to me

that she wanted a coffee. I told the waitress that we weren't ready.

'Lily, you've got to be able to order for yourself. It's no good looking at me. How will you eat and drink if you can't ask for anything?'

'But I don't know what to say. How can I speak Japanese? I don't know anything at all.'

I found her wimpishness irritating but at the same time felt a sisterly protectiveness. She was helpless.

'I bet you do. There are some Japanese words that everyone knows. How about shogun?'

'Oh, OK. Yes, I've heard of that. I don't know what it is, though. Origami. I know that one. Or is that Chinese? No, it's Japanese, isn't it. Is it? I don't know.'

'It's Japanese. Kamikaze?'

'Yes. Those pilots in the war. Erm. Sumo. Karaoke. Futon.'

'See. You do know some.'

'Karate. Noodle.'

'That's not Japanese. There are lots of words for noodles. I'll teach you some time. I want tea and you want coffee, right?'

'Right.'

'So tea is *kohcha* and coffee is *koohii*.'

'*Kohcha. Koohii,*' she repeated with a strong Yorkshire o.

'Yes. Now, when you want to say "one" you add *hitotsu.*'

'*Hitotsu kohcha—*'

'No. *Kohcha o hitotsu. Koohii o hitotsu.*'

'So it goes backwards. What's "o"?'

'It's just a particle. It doesn't really mean anything—'

'So why do I need to say it?'

'You just do. Are you ready?' I was never meant to be a teacher.

'No, wait. Let me have a little practice first. *Kohcha o hitotsu. Koohii o hitotsu.* How do I say "please"?'

'Just add *kudasai* on the end. OK, I'm calling the waitress.'

Lily said her piece to the waitress who, fortunately, understood.

'Wow. Me speaking Japanese. Wait till Andy finds out.'

'I thought you weren't in touch with him any more.'

'No, I'm not. He doesn't know that I'm here. Hardly anyone knows. I don't want to see him

again but at the same time, I don't believe I never
will.'

'How come?'

'He was so possessive, as I said. I think he'll
either track me down and come after me or
he'll meet someone else and be obsessive about her
instead.'

'That would be better.'

'Didn't you say before that you had a boyfriend?
What's his name?'

'Teiji.'

'Is he a translator too?'

'He's a photographer. Well, he works in a noodle
shop.'

'But he wants to be a photographer. Brilliant. I
love taking photographs but I'm not very good.
I like pictures of views – you know, sunsets and
that. I wish I had a camera here now. Does he sell
his pictures or what?'

'No. I don't think so. I don't know.'

'But he will in the future?'

'I'm not sure.'

'But it's a hobby. So he can put them on the
walls to brighten them up, and give them to people
and stuff. That's nice.'

Why did Teiji take photographs? He gave a few

of them to me but mostly he did nothing with them. I realized it must have sounded odd to Lily but I didn't want to talk about it with her.

'Do you think you'll stay in Japan long?'

'I don't know. It's funny because I've only been here a couple of weeks, but I'm a bit homesick. There are things I miss that I probably wouldn't even want if I was back at home now. Do you find that?'

'This is home now so all I can think of is how homesick I would be if I ever left Japan.'

'I miss fish and chips. And shops where I can buy what I want. I've noticed the shoes here are all too small for me. I could just do with a walk down Whitefriargate to look at shoes.'

'That's true. With my big feet I have a shoe problem too.'

'Do you miss the Yorkshire coast?'

'No.'

'There must be something about it you like.'

'There is. Erosion. That part of the coast has some of the worst erosion in the world. It's falling into the sea as we speak. A foot or two every year falls off the edge and drowns itself. Or swims southward and becomes part of East Anglia. That's something I like.'

'I went to the seaside when I was a kid. We used to go at weekends. I remember paddling in the sea till my skin went blue. And there were those huge waves that knocked you over. I hated the cold but I did like being in water.'

Lucy was jolted into the past and missed whatever Lily said next. Lucy was swimming, trying to go fast enough to keep warm when she felt furry hands stroking and clinging to her legs. At first she thought it was one of her seven brothers, a prank, but the touch was feminine and insistent like the caressing fingers of a mermaid. She thought it was pulling her down, under the waves to drown her, but not violently, softly and quietly. A couple of minutes later she was kneeling in shallow waves. Dark, heavy seaweed was wrapped around both legs.

'I liked eating candyfloss at the beach,' Lucy heard Lily say.

'I did, too. I loved candyfloss.'

'And ice creams, but the sand always blew in and stuck to it.'

We finished our drinks in silence. I had goose bumps from the air-conditioning. When we went back into the warm humidity, I was disorientated to find myself in Tokyo.

'Never thought I'd be in Japan,' Lily said, removing her cardigan. 'If you'd've asked me a year ago I wouldn't've found it on a map.'

I should have walked away then. She knew how to get home. But something occurred to me and I stupidly opened my mouth and shared it with Lily.

'I'm going hiking on Sunday with Natsuko – she's a colleague – and I think you'd like her. It's not a particularly difficult hike but should be quite interesting. You might want to come.'

Lily was lost, lonely, out of her depth, in need of kindness. I knew that. Let me explain why I was so unwilling to spend time with her. It was because of another story, a story that I didn't tell Lily. And one that I'm not telling the police. I told only Teiji. I told Teiji once and once is enough to tell the story of one's life.

This is how it happened. I lay between the covers of Teiji's bed. He slipped in beside me, warmed my bare skin with his, held his camera at arm's length, pointed it and took a picture of us. It was one of the few photographs he took that included his own image. He tossed the camera aside and whispered something. What did he whisper? It seems to me now that Teiji and I never used words, but of course we must have. I remember times when I'm sure we were talking but I cannot recall a syllable of what we said. I have a sense that feelings and ideas passed between us like telepathy but that is too fanciful. I can't hear Teiji's voice but he must have had a voice. If I concentrate then what I hear is a sound like the patter of raindrops coming from our mouths. No pauses, no turn-taking, just water falling. I can't be sure of his exact words, but this is what I believe he said that evening.

'How did you get here?'

I resisted the temptation to say, 'I took the Yamanote line and then I walked,' for I knew that was not the answer to his question.

'I don't know,' I said.

'But you're here, in Japan. I found you. You came to Japan from another land, another continent, so far away, and I found you in my camera. How?'

And I told him. I started from the beginning and told him almost everything.

Three

I began with my birth.

Lucy Fly was born in Scarborough in 1965, in a Victorian terraced house with severe grey brickwork and three solid steps up to the front door. The North Sea wind blew so hard against the door that you needed to put on a coat and hat just to put the milk bottles out. Lucy was the youngest of eight children belonging to George and Miriam Fly, and the only girl. She was born at home, in darkness. The bedroom lightbulb went out with a pop just as the midwife urged Miriam to give a final push. George was downstairs watching the rugby league but tore himself graciously away for long enough to replace the bulb with the one from the outside bog. When finally she could see, Miriam, the very proud mother of seven sons, stared miserably at the red mess that was lifted from the aching gap between her legs. She had been waiting for her eighth son. He would have been called Jonah.

'Very fitting,' George had said under his breath the week before, 'since he'll be springing forth from a great whale.'

But all Miriam could see was a boy without a willy.

'It's a lovely girl!' said the midwife, wiping the baby clean.

Miriam did not see the loveliness. She saw a scrawny pink girl with no neck and beady black crow's eyes. It hadn't ever occurred to her that she could produce a girl. She was an efficient male-producing factory and considered it her right to be so. Miriam wasn't a cruel person but her own childhood had been blighted by its lack of any men. Her father had died during the war. She had two sisters, no brothers and, to compound the unfairness, she was forced to attend all-girls schools. The only men she spoke to were bus conductors and the coal man. She wanted a man who would pick her up, tell her she was a little princess. Miriam's suffering was rewarded in adulthood. She claimed her rightful place at the centre of male attention and her seven sons were part of the entitlement.

'Oh well,' she said, feeling the pain at the core of her and knowing this was the last baby she would have. 'Some help folding the bedsheets. Crow's eyes or not.'

Such was Miriam's admirable stoicism in the face of overwhelming disappointment. She thought, at first, of naming the baby Linda, meaning beautiful. That was the name she had wanted as a child. But the paradox was cruel and so, at the midwife's suggestion, the baby girl was named Lucy, which means light, because George was on a chair changing a lightbulb when Lucy flopped out. He left the room immediately and without looking, to let the women do their things with blood and warm water. He awaited the news downstairs.

'A girl?' His face showed genuine surprise. 'Bugger me.'

There is no evidence of elucidation of this remark. At any rate, life for George and Miriam did not change so much. They still had shepherd's pie for tea on Tuesdays, and fish fingers on Fridays. A girl could wear boys' clothes, for the most part, and didn't seem to need any special treatment. She toddled around learning things for herself and keeping out of the way of her brothers, who didn't see the point of her, though she made a good cannonball when they wanted to test the glass of the greenhouse. Little Lucy was not much good to Miriam, even as an assistant, because she was so clumsy. She broke the dishes she washed and dropped hot plates coming from the oven. She couldn't cook, no matter how hard she tried.

Miriam grunted. 'How will you ever get married if you can't make pastry? You'll never get anywhere, mark my words.'

'I will,' said Lucy, with the voice inside her head that always said the same thing, 'I'll get away from here.'

But when Lucy was seven they moved away from Scarborough and it was worse. The family moved to a small town further down the coast so that Miriam could complain about being isolated. Unlike Scarborough, this town had no cliffs, no hills. It was flat and empty. There was nothing else to do but go to the beach. Every Sunday they ate sandy picnics in the eye-watering wind, swam in the rough, cold North Sea. The seven brothers played Death on the breakwater while Lucy preferred to go up to a bench on the promenade and read a book. It was too windy even there, but it was better than being thrown onto the jagged wooden breakwater and having all your skin pulled off. Miriam did not approve.

'We come all this way and spend money on a house by the sea and you go and stick your big beak in some book. You think you're too good for us. You're not. You're just allergic to fresh air.'

The North Sea became Lucy's first enemy. George told her that at the other side lay Norway. And if you dug a hole in the sand, and kept digging, you'd come out in Australia standing on your head. Lucy decided that of the two options, Norway was the more realistic. One east coast summer's afternoon, when the sea and sky were grey and the wind swept the beach, Lucy set off. She lay on the family lilo and paddled as fast as she could, knowing that all she had to do was not fall off and not get swept back. The North Sea was having none of this. It rocked and pushed. Finally it tipped her over so that she was clinging to the underneath of the lilo with a mouth full of salt water. Her feet didn't touch the bottom and for the first time in her short life she felt panic. But the monster was not going to gobble Lucy up. She swam as fast as she could and reached the shore several minutes before the lilo. No one had noticed her absence, but then it was rare that they ever noticed her presence.

The seven brothers hardly spoke to Lucy. Miriam didn't like them to. Somehow she felt that it would belittle them to give their attentions to a small girl instead of their mother. To Miriam, the seven sons were angels. They were not. They were pigs who threw water bombs from behind doors, emptied spud guns in the eyes of neighbourhood children, wiped their arses on the bathroom towels when it was too much trouble to find the end of the toilet paper.

For Lucy, the misfortune of having seven such older brothers was not relieved even when one of them – Noah, the nastiest of all – died. Since Miriam continued to refer to her seven sons when there were only six, it was hard for Lucy to see Noah's death as much of an achievement. She did, however, have some claim in its coming about.

It happened on a bright day in the summer holidays in the shade of the biggest apple tree in the garden. When Lucy was seven or eight, this was the best tree for climbing. She was large enough to lever herself up the trunk but not too big to endanger the thinner branches. The trunk divided into two, like a pair of legs in a wobbly handstand.

Either leg could be climbed but Lucy liked the one
that stretched over the lawn. She could crawl along
it and jump onto the soft grass below. Lucy had
no fear and was happy to fling herself from the top.
Sometimes, to make it harder, she stuck objects –
a pitchfork, a couple of garden spades, sharp
planks of wood – into the grass to leap beyond.
And when that lost its ability to challenge Lucy,
she began to jump backwards. She sustained many
scrapes, bruises and gashes those long summers,
but she could not stop herself.

When she didn't feel like jumping, Lucy would
crawl along to the end of the bough and sit in a
nook of branches, watching the world beneath.
Lucy liked observation points, not so much
because she liked to watch but because, in a carefully chosen position, she could be fairly sure that
no one was observing her. Sometimes she took a
book. *Pippi Longstocking* and *The Secret Garden*
were her favourites. She admired feisty Pippi and
empathized with miserable Mary who'd lived in
India and ended up in Yorkshire.

On that cloudless day Lucy was reading *Polly-
anna*. A teacher had lent it to her but so far she
was disgusted. This drippy girl didn't know how
to complain but looked for good things everywhere

when clearly they were bad. Lucy stopped every few pages to rearrange herself in the branches and to shake the tree to see if she could turn any loose apples into windfalls. The seven brothers appeared, back from a fishing trip with the Boy Scouts. They were delighted to spot Lucy in her crow's nest over the garden. At the command of Noah, they surrounded the apple tree and pounded it with stones to knock their sister to the ground. Lucy knew that if she jumped down they would get her. But if she stayed on her perch she might very well be stoned to death, like St Stephen. She could become a Christian martyr but that was no good because she'd decided some years before that she was an atheist. If she screamed for help nothing at all would happen because Miriam was running a jumble sale at the town hall and George was never around. Lucy saw on the grass a sharper, heavier stone than the ones hitting her arms and legs. It had multiple angles that would cut your fingers just holding it. If you threw it, you could probably kill an elephant by cutting its head right off. And before she had finished noticing the stone, there was a hand on it. Noah's fat fingers had grasped the weapon and were lifting it from the grass. He looked up at her with pale blue eyes full of bubbling malice. Lucy pulled herself back a little on the long bough. As Noah's arm came up, poised to throw, she pushed down with all her might. She sprang out of the tree in a perfect trajectory and landed on Noah. Noah fell back and was impaled between the shoulder-blades on a long rusty nail sticking out of one of Lucy's planks of wood. He sat up with the plank attached to his back and for once was speechless. Then he fell again and let the stone slip from his grasp. His curly blond hair was pasted to his forehead with sweat. His eyes were open, still staring at Lucy. He died in hospital that night.

I will not recall the devastation of this act upon the parents of this beautiful young boy. It is enough to say that Lucy did not bother to bother anyone in the family after that and kept herself to herself, though she did not like to sit in her tree any more. She had only meant to squash Noah, not to puncture him. Eventually, and against the wishes of the town council, George chopped the cooking apple tree down, hacked it into pieces, and burned it in a crackling orange bonfire. Did the smoke billow and make tears gather at the corners of his eyes? Lucy never knew. She wasn't watching.

Lucy didn't speak for the next three years. The last person she talked to was the kind nurse who took her away from the hospital ward, holding her small hand tightly, along a corridor that smelt of sick and disinfectant. She said to Lucy, 'You understand that it's not your fault, don't you?'

And Lucy answered, 'Yes, no, yes,' because she didn't understand the question and didn't know which answer the nice nurse wanted to hear.

She did not, could not utter a word after that and life was much simpler. At home they either didn't notice or were relieved. The seven (six) brothers had lost their appetite for Lucy's blood since the accident. At school the teachers left her alone; after all, there were bound to be a couple of odd ones in every year. The other children whispered about her but never came too close because they knew she could kill so easily. Three silent, blissful years passed. Then she won the county junior chess contest.

The local newspaper had prepared a piece about Lucy the Tragic Mute Genius. There is one thing above all that Lucy has never been able to tolerate and that is presumption about Lucy. So complacent, so unquestioning, they wrote their fantasy about her loneliness, her reach for chess as a desperate last hope of communication with the world. Lucy had taken up chess precisely because there was no need to speak. *Check* can be communicated with the eyes and eyebrows. If some pedant insists on the use of the word, it can be written on the back of the hand. So at the prize-giving ceremony she opened her mouth and spoke clearly but casually into the microphone, 'Thanks,' as if she had been speaking every day. Checkmate. Except that she had only cornered herself. Once she had spoken again, it was impossible to rediscover the silence.

At secondary school, Lucy made a friend, her first and only friend until she left home at eighteen. Her name was Lizzie. Although Lucy was speaking now, the other children had long ago pronounced her weird. Lucy accepted weirdness as her definition and quite naturally took to her role of friend to other weirdos. Lizzie was as gangly as Lucy was stumpy. Even at eleven, she was as tall as the tallest teachers. She had long, lank hair and a thin, sad face. They made each other look stranger but they had plenty in common. Lucy played the cello and Lizzie the trombone. Sometimes they played together during the ten-minute breaks between lessons. They would find a corner of a classroom or the playground and play simple duets based on pieces stolen from the school orchestra, or songs they heard on the radio. They were a freak show and, naturally, people stared, sneered, sometimes teased. But no one ever tried to stop them.

They had nothing to complain about. They enjoyed being left on their own. Name-calling from these bumpkins couldn't wound. They made many attempts at inventing their own language, though they usually failed. But in French lessons they bounded ahead of the other pupils. Lucy and Lizzie read Asterix books, copied words out of their French dictionaries, spoke together in French. Where they didn't know the vocabulary or grammar, they invented it and pronounced it with French accents copied from Debbie Harry on *Top of the Pops*. They truly believed they were speaking French, though now Lucy wonders if any French person would have understood a word they said.

But it was not enough to satisfy Lucy. (Was anything?) The secret language was not sufficiently secret to guarantee total separation from others. And anyway, Lizzie was always taking time off school because she thought she was sick. Over the years she contracted cancer, arthritis, lumbago, flu, meningitis, gout, dengue fever and more. Lucy knew Lizzie couldn't have had all of them but she suffered as though she did. Lucy was as strong as an ox and lonely without her friend.

While Lizzie's imagination travelled through the pages of a medical dictionary, Lucy's fervour was for the atlas. She kept the meagre family map and atlas collection under her bed with a torch. She studied a country every night, its mountain ranges, rivers and, most of all, its language. A school trip to the British Museum led to Lucy's epiphany. She saw the Rosetta Stone for the first time, and realized the weak point of her education. The Roman alphabet. While the other teenagers chattered around her, Lucy stared at the stone. The hieroglyphics tantalized her with their hidden meaning but she knew there was a message there for her. The message was that she should learn a language that no one she knew would be able to read, never mind speak.

Lucy left Yorkshire and went to London to study Japanese. She chose London because after enduring her small town at the edge of England it didn't occur to her that there could be anything better than its exact opposite, the capital. She selected Japanese after some deliberation. Chinese required the study of over six thousand characters whereas Japanese used a paltry two to three thousand. On that point China was in the lead. But the map won the day. Japan was slightly further away from England and that was an important consideration. Japan was almost as far as you could go without starting to slip round the globe toward home again, unless you went to Australia, but that didn't count because they spoke English. There were no tears, only relief on all sides. Most of the brothers had left home and this had pushed Lucy and Miriam uncomfortably close. George had died of grief for Noah two years before, in the arms of a woman who wasn't Miriam, and that was that.

At university Lucy made the exciting discovery that her body ran most efficiently not on her previous diet of fish fingers, Eccles cakes or even raw cooking apples, but on a regular intake of alcohol and sperm. It made her healthier, happier and more intelligent. She went for men who were already drunk when they met her, for they would not be put off by her strange eyes. She found that her eyes gave the drunkard something to focus on. Her academic grades soared. It became easier and easier to learn the kanji and fun to practise writing them out. After three years and a lot of sex, Lucy could barely remember the names of the seven (six) brothers and considered herself ready to graduate.

She didn't contact Miriam. She decided she would only speak to her mother if Miriam called or wrote first. Miriam never did. So when Lucy left her cosy hall of residence and set off for Japan, there was no need for an explanation.

She found a flat and worked for several companies, editing documents, translating presentations and instruction manuals. Finally, four years ago, she settled in her current position. She became a translator and editor for a small industrial translation company. With no understanding of engineering, electronics, or even electricity – though she was born under a changing lightbulb – Lucy spent her days putting Japanese sentences into English, twisting the words so that the end went at the beginning, articles and plurals appeared, vagaries became specifics.

And here my story drew toward its happy conclusion.

Tokyo was more than Lucy could have hoped for. Too big ever to be found there, too noisy to have to listen to anything, too expensive to worry about saving any money. And under the chaos, a cool and quietly beating heart. An organ that pumped blood through stooping centenarians, three-year-old Nintendo whizz-kids, office workers with no time for meals or sleep, and university students with all the time in the world.

Teiji was asleep before I'd finished. Actually, he fell asleep just after I'd started. I knew, but I didn't stop because I saw that my story was becoming a nice lullaby for him. I didn't think it rude of him to sleep; he had realized as soon as I'd started to speak that his question was not going to be answered, at least not that day. And it was all for the best. If he'd known I was a child murderer, he might not have loved me any more.

Four

Kameyama puts his elbows on the desk, clasps his hands under his chin.

'I've asked you the same question ten times. Let me put it to you again. Why did you argue with Lily Bridges? What had happened to cause the incident witnessed by your neighbour?'

'I was angry. I told you.'

'Why?'

I don't want to lie. I like to be truthful but any truths I tell will get me into trouble, and so honesty is out of the question.

'Nothing much. Some trivial thing.'

The day I went flat-hunting with Lily left me uncomfortable. She had reminded me of my childhood and caused me to wonder where I was. Teiji arrived at my flat early that evening. A few hours had passed since I'd parted with Lily and I was almost grounded again in Tokyo. Lily was beginning to seem like a strange ghost from the past. I couldn't understand why I'd mentioned the hike. I regretted inviting her and hoped it would rain so the trip would be cancelled.

Teiji took a shower. I listened to the water pouring over his body, occasional knocks and clinks as he reached for soap or shampoo, his feet on the floor when he climbed out. I heard the towel rub back and forth across his neck, back, legs. He cleared his throat a couple of times. The plughole gurgled and the bathroom door opened. I looked up at him. Water slipped from his black hair as if it had lost the power to be wet, as if it were droplets of mercury. A couple of rubs with the towel and his hair was almost dry. And then he came to me and rested his head in my lap. He looked up at me with one eye as I stroked his hair. The other eye was squashed against my thigh. He reached out one arm and groped around on the floor for his camera. His fingers touched it. He lifted it and, without moving his head, looked up at my face through the viewfinder, clicked the silver button, smiled at me. He hung the camera round his neck, where it belonged. I leaned over and kissed him.

But Lily's words were heavy in my thoughts and I couldn't force myself not to speak of them.

'Teiji, why do you take so many photographs? You don't sell them. You don't even put them on your walls.'

He was quiet for a moment. Then, 'Don't you like them? I try to give you ones I think you'll like.'

Teiji's voice is coming back to me, faintly, but it's there in my ears.

'Yes, thank you, I do. But there are so many more. I don't understand why.'

'I just take them. It's a habit.'

'But there's no final purpose?'

'I'm collecting them.'

'For what?'

'My collection.'

'Teiji, what *is* your collection?'

'All my photographs.'

He moved to sit behind me with his legs around mine. The camera swung forward and hit the back of my head.

'Do you want me to stop taking photographs?'

'No.' I wished I hadn't started this. Damn Lily, making me question the very thing that had drawn me to Teiji. He had no answers for me. I knew that already.

'Because I wouldn't.'

'I know.'

'Why are we talking about this?'

'I don't want you to stop taking pictures at all. I just wonder why you don't try to do something with them.'

'Such as?'

'I don't know. Such as selling them.'

'I don't need to. If I needed the money, I'd sell them, but I don't because I have a good job that pays me enough money.'

Teiji dashed off an hour later to do the evening shift at the restaurant. I was left feeling foolish for starting such a stupid conversation. But something was still bothering me, and it wasn't just Lily's questions about what Teiji should do with his pictures. It was the thought of those two boxes in his flat. Stacks and stacks of photographs that recounted years of his life, perhaps back to his very first camera. He never showed me any of them. I couldn't see why and I couldn't stop wondering about it. He sometimes gave me pictures containing images of Lucy, but nothing from before Lucy. I knew so little about Teiji.

What *did* I know? That destiny led Teiji both to photography and to the noodle shop. I knew certain facts about him. He grew up near Kagoshima on the southern edge of Kyushu, the southernmost of Japan's biggest islands. He was born in the shadow of Sakurajima, an active volcano on its own island, that spewed dark smoke and rumbled deeply like a far-off highway at nighttime. Until he was nine years old he thought that it was normal for mountains to behave in such a manner and lived in hope only of seeing a glorious eruption one day. In the meantime, he spent his days whizzing through the countryside on an old bicycle. His mother made his lunch. She pressed hot rice into fat triangles, pushed a sour plum into the centre of each, and covered them in dark seaweed. When they had cooled, he stuffed them into his pockets and set off along the country roads, careering this way and that, but with the volcanic island never far from sight. To celebrate his first day at junior high school, Teiji's father gave him an old camera. Teiji took it with him on his long bike journeys. It hung around his neck and bumped up and down as he cycled. He shot pictures of the volcano from every angle.

His other favourite subject was water. He would

wander to the sea's edge and take off his shoes to paddle. Teiji could never quite believe in water or smoke and felt sure that if he photographed them, they would not appear in the picture. He took photos of his toes through the water's rippling surface, expecting to see an image only of his toes. When the pictures were developed he rushed to the shop to collect them. Then he took them to the sea to compare the image with reality. Sometimes he could not decide which was the image and which was real. He knew he would have to take more pictures until he found the answer. Soon he forgot the volcano island, though it was always there, making smoke, sending it out and up into the sky.

When Teiji was fourteen his father died. Teiji and his mother moved to Tokyo where his mother's brother ran a noodle shop. His mother began to work there and Teiji helped out at weekends. He was slender but he was strong and proved helpful in moving delivery crates, lifting furniture to sweep the floor. But he could not rest without the sea and often walked down to Tokyo Bay. The water there was grey in the day and black at night. He wandered through corridors of concrete and neon, confused by the hugeness of the buildings, the number of people. The city moved like thick, dirty water but Teiji could not find its source. He walked the streets night and day, hoping to capture an answer with his camera. At seventeen he dropped out of high school and went to work full-time in the noodle shop. He spoke little to his mother and uncle, but he worked hard and no one complained about him. Then his mother died.

This is the story Teiji had told me on another dark night, with a few embellishments of my own. There is much that he never shared. Did he miss his mother? Perhaps. The boxes in his room contained photographs of his whole life. But he never showed them to me and now that I was finally finding the courage to steal a secret look in those treasure chests, I planned to search for something else. I didn't see the pictures that told of his childhood.

Those were the stories in my head. Who can say where I got them from? At first they were enough – he was the magical statue I found in Shinjuku and he was perfect – but now I wanted more. There were many missing years. I wanted to see his photographs, open up the boxes.

Of course, once you have had the idea, it is impossible to lose it again. I knew that I would see the pictures so I decided to save myself hours or weeks of agonizing and do it immediately. About twenty minutes after Teiji had gone, I set off for his flat. He kept a spare key in a crack in the wall beside his front door. I fished it out and let myself in.

I went straight to the boxes. I was nervous. In some ways his room belonged to me – I knew every nook and cranny, every speck and stain – but in other respects it was forbidden territory. Beneath the cardboard flaps were envelopes and folders full of pictures, all in neat piles. The first box held the pictures of his childhood. I wasn't so interested in those for the moment. I closed the box and pushed it back against the wall. The contents of the other box were a chronicle of his life since arriving in Tokyo. Toward the top were the pictures he'd taken of me. I imagined the bottom ones were his earlier treasures, his last days at high school, first days in the restaurant. I dug for the middle layer. I didn't want to know about his arrival here. I wanted to know about the in-between Tokyo years, the ones before he met Lucy.

There were the usual pictures of water, of pavement scenes, of train stations and tunnels. Then I found what I suppose I had been looking for. A picture of a young woman. She was looking at the camera through the window of a bus. She had a soft, round face, deeply set eyes and hair cut into a bob which brushed her chin. She looked as if she could have been pretty but she glowered at the camera through tired, angry eyes. Was this Teiji's lover before he found me?

There were more pictures. I followed her backward through them until I found the first. I was excited by what I saw. She was on stage in a play. The picture must have been taken from the back of the theatre for she was just a small figure under the lights. She was wearing a soldier's uniform and had a gun over her shoulder. Her mouth was open in a silent shout. The stage was small and she was the only actor. The walls of the theatre were black. I wondered at Teiji's being there. Had he gone there because he knew her, or was he there because he wanted to see the play and then he happened to find her? He'd never mentioned any interest in theatre, but if he'd met her before, there should have been an earlier photograph. Prior to the soldier, there was nothing, just a few shots of a man in the noodle shop smiling stiffly through damp, red eyes at the camera.

I followed her forward again. There were several

more pictures taken in theatres. She was in different costumes but it was hard to make out her face. There were other pictures: coffee shops, parks, a riverside, parties. As I went through them I saw that there were fewer and fewer where she was an actress and more where she was at parties, sitting on worn tatami or on a bed. Her face became fatter and paler through the pictures. Then there were only parties. She came to look sad and then sadder. Her tight-fitting clothes were crumpled and stained. The last one I had a chance to see showed the woman lying on her front on a pavement, head to one side. The corners of her mouth were raised. She might have been grimacing or smiling. I couldn't tell. I wondered what on earth she was doing. She must have been drunk.

'They're private.'

Teiji's voice was flat. He had entered the room without a noise – or I had been too engrossed to hear it – and stood behind me.

I had no answer. I was caught red-handed. The only thing I could say was sorry, but I really wasn't sorry that I'd looked, only that I'd been caught. I stood but couldn't face Teiji.

'I know. I shouldn't have looked.'

'We didn't have any customers, so I got the evening off. I was going to call you.'

I shrugged. 'Now you don't need to.'

'No. I don't.' He walked round in front of me, looked into my eyes.

I thought I'd blown it. He didn't say anything for a few moments. Now that I'd seen this woman, the actress, he looked different to me. His eyes seemed darker, his hair thicker, his bones more clearly defined. He had come into focus, somehow. I stared back, waited for him to speak.

'Let's stay in. Come on.' With one foot he pushed the open box to the corner of the room. He pulled me to the bed and sat beside me. There was an expression of sadness on his face when he held my chin and looked at me. I think he felt bad for catching me out. He was probably angry but he was also sorry for me. He watched me for minutes. I didn't know what he was looking for, but I was worried of what he might see.

I couldn't get the scowling woman out of my head. I needed to ask.

'Who was she?'

'Sachi.'

'Where is she now?'

'I don't know. She's gone.'

'She just went all of a sudden?'

'We finished. She left. I don't try to find her.' He sighed deeply. 'Lucy, I found you and I don't think of Sachi any more.'

I didn't speak. It was hard to believe he didn't think of her any more when I was sure I would never stop thinking of her.

'When something's gone, it's gone. You look for the next thing. I found you.'

We made love but I was unable to enjoy it. I felt guilty because I'd broken into Teiji's flat, guiltier still because he was showing no anger. And mostly I couldn't enjoy it because I was looking at Sachi's unhappy face, all the time.

The next morning was bright and sunny so the hike wouldn't be cancelled. Lucy was now glad. It would be good to see other people, good to get away from Teiji and Sachi. I was still wary of Lily but that feeling was almost cancelled by my desire to see Natsuko. Smiling, always calm, sometimes bossy, Natsuko.

Natsuko was my first friend in Tokyo. She was the second friend in Lucy's life, after the long-faced, trombone-playing Lizzie. We worked together when I first arrived. When Natsuko found a better job with another company, she worked as hard as she could to ensure a job there for me. It took more than three years and we have both been there ever since. Natsuko is about my age and is bilingual. She speaks English with an accent that is sometimes Australian and sometimes American because she travelled so much as a child. Occasionally she sounds German and from time to time Irish. She has a round, dimpled face and even when she is not smiling her lips are set in the form of a smile. I have often wondered at it. She looks perpetually happy, in the way that I look perpetually gloomy, for even when I smile, my mouth does not always move. It is an effort to draw my lips into a smile to keep people happy, when in fact I am perfectly content inside.

We had our lunch together every day. Bentos of rice, fish, seaweed, cans of green tea. Sometimes we chatted about work, about our weekends. Often we didn't find any conversation to make, but we still sat together because that was good enough. Once a month or so we went out into the mountains together and hiked for a day. On the way down we would stop at a hot spring, strip off, and let our tired muscles tingle in steamy water.

I regarded Natsuko as a constant. She never

asked me about my private life. Sometimes she told me of hers – a series of unsatisfactory boyfriends, her desperation to move out of her parents' house though she couldn't afford to rent a flat – and left a space open for me to volunteer titbits of my own life. I just didn't. Not because I didn't trust Natsuko or felt uncomfortable. I loved everything she was. I didn't want to spoil it by talking about myself.

Natsuko helped me when I joined the company and she was there beside me every day. She lent me pencils and dictionaries. She taught me new kanji and Japanese slang. Now she is not so sure about Lucy. She probably wonders why I never talked about myself, what I was hiding from her, and so she avoids me. I don't mind being ignored. It can remove many obstacles and irritations of daily life. But I can't deny that I am a little disappointed in Natsuko.

However, in those days she was good to me. She helped me find my job, and she also found the string quartet, for which I will always be grateful.

I arrived at Shinjuku. It was early morning but the station was already alive. People in suits boarded trains for work, though it was a weekend. A few people in crushed, smoky work clothes headed home from the previous night's fun looking tired and shrivelled. I passed a group of chattering high-school students who carried kendo swords in cases over their shoulders. I looked for Lily, half-hoping that she had overslept. But she was there, with Natsuko and a couple of other people. Lily had invited Bob. Bob had brought his colleague, Richard. Natsuko was in the middle of the throng, busily introducing herself to the others, beaming.

'Hi, Lucy. I'm so glad you invited all these people. It's going to be so much fun.'

She sounded Australian today. She'd lived in Melbourne between the ages of six and ten. Any activity that was fun or energetic brought back her Australian accent. At work she tended to sound American. I guessed it was because she went to university and studied translation in New York.

'Hi, Luce,' said Bob. 'So you're going to lead the expedition into the mountains? Hope you've brought supplies in case we get lost.'

'Don't joke,' I said. 'You don't know me well enough. There's more than a little chance that if I were in charge here we'd all go over the edge of a precipice, or perish in a freak landslide. Disaster is always at my heels. No, Natsuko is our navigator for the day and a very good one too. She knows all the best routes and the hidden tracks away from the crowds.'

'It's a clear day so we should get some good views,' Natsuko said. 'I can't wait to get up there. I need the exercise too. I've been drinking like a fish for the past month and I'm almost bursting out of my Lycra.'

She lifted her T-shirt a few inches to prove this and laughed. Richard and Bob immediately pulled their clothes around to display their own ample midriffs. Amid the boasting and teasing a weedy voice piped up.

'Will we see Mount Fuji?'

I had forgotten Lily. I was surprised she had heard of Mount Fuji but I supposed that it only took a few weeks in Japan to pick up certain facts.

'Yes, I hope so.' Natsuko showed her map to Lily. 'See. There are a couple of viewing points on the trail. If it's clear we'll see it at least twice. You ought to see Fuji, you know. It'll be a kind of initiation for you. Does everyone have plenty of water and something for lunch?'

She herded us to the train. The carriage was full of other hikers heading out in the same direction. Most were middle-aged or elderly. When Natsuko and I went to the mountains, we rarely saw other people under the age of forty. That morning was typical. There were all-female groups and a few mixed parties, none made up only of men. They had expensive-looking walking gear – Gore-tex shoes, mountain sticks, shiny rucksacks and hiking hats. The women wore round hats with floppy brims. The men had peaked caps.

Our group was less professionally attired. We sported a mixture of jeans and leggings, old trainers, baggy T-shirts and no hats, though Richard wore a red bandanna. I was pleased Bob and Richard had come. I was in a solitary mood and it is much easier to be alone in a large group than in a threesome. Natsuko was in her element as mother hen, showing Lily the map and explaining where we were going.

The mountains in Yamanashi were soft and green, with air that smelled of soil, rain and pine trees. I had been breathing the Tokyo air that smelled of people and traffic for months. When we arrived at the base of our mountain, I felt lightheaded.

'I love the countryside,' Lily said, coming to stand beside me. 'Doesn't it make you feel like a kid again? We used to go walking, Andy and me, in the Yorkshire Moors and on the Dales. It's beautiful.'

I withheld a scream. Why did she have to keep going on about that damned place? How could I concentrate on being in Yamanashi if she was going to dredge up various parts of Yorkshire with every comment? I gave her remark a perfunctory nod and went to find Bob. We walked together until the mountain became steep. There were old farmhouses here and there with gardens full of bright flowers and thick green trees.

'I think,' Bob said, 'Lily's settling in. Thanks to you.'

'I really haven't done anything. Finding the flat was easy.'

'She's more confident now. And learning Japanese too. She said you started her off.'

'Well, she needed to be able to say something at least. God knows, she talks enough in English.'

Bob smiled. 'You're a good Japanese teacher. You certainly helped me with a tricky situation at the dentist's. How are your teeth?'

'Just fine. Yours?'

'A bit more treatment to go. Soon be over, though. These trees are beautiful.'

We had left the roads and houses and were now

on a dirt path surrounded by tall pines. They stood silent and still, like breathing statues. We began to climb. A stream ran along beside us for much of the way and a couple of times we had to cross it. Bob and I helped each other over, then waited for the others. As the climbing became tougher, the chattering declined to occasional comments, then silence apart from the sound of breath and feet. That is my favourite part of a hike, when all the words and sentences have been talked out of you and people slip, one by one, into their own thoughts and dreams.

After a couple of hours we arrived at a low peak. We could see for miles around. Distant mountains and valleys, small villages and paddy fields. Natsuko consulted her book.

'We should be able to see Mount Fuji in that direction.' She pointed to a range of higher mountains, covered with blue sky. We clustered around but could see no sign of Fuji.

'It's big enough,' Richard said. 'If it was there, we'd see it. The book must be wrong.'

'No,' Bob looked through his binoculars, 'it's just too hazy. I think Fuji's hiding from us today.'

Lily put one hand on my shoulder and pointed with the other. 'What's that?'

I looked. Above the tops of the other mountains was empty space. But higher in the sky, as if suspended in it, was the unmistakable cone of Fuji's peak. There seemed to be no mountain below it, just the silhouette of the peak sitting in the sky.

'It's like a ghost,' I said.

'Can mountains have ghosts?' Natsuko asked.

'I don't know.'

Richard sat on the ledge, opened his rucksack for lunch. 'Why not? It's a dead volcano. If it can be dead, why can't it have a ghost?'

'It's extinct. That's not exactly the same as dead. Dead has a personal, individual connotation, worthy of ghosts,' Bob, as an English teacher, pointed out.

'In Japanese it's the same. The word for extinct volcano is *shikazan*. It means dead volcano, or dead fire mountain. I don't see why it shouldn't have a ghost of itself.' Natsuko shielded her eyes from the sun to see better.

'I think you'll find it's a trick of the light,' Bob said.

'We know,' said Natsuko. 'But we want to think of it as a ghost. Look at it hovering up there. It is spooky, supernatural. When I move away from my parents' house and into a place of my own, I want to have a view of Mount Fuji. That's the most important thing for me. I'd like to be able to look out and see it every day. That's all I want. If I had that, I'm sure I'd be happy for ever.'

I smiled at her, turned to the peak in the sky. One by one the others had enough of the view and settled on the ground for lunch. Lucy could not take her eyes from it and wondered what kind of picture Teiji would take if he were there. It was a view that could have been designed for Teiji. Lucy could hardly believe that he wasn't with her. Then she remembered the photographs in the box and her face burned.

'It's private,' he had said. 'I don't think about her any more.'

Sachi. I would think about her for ever. Her angry eyes, the face that became whiter and puffier with each photograph. The parties where she looked drawn and unamused, always away from other people, wearing dirty, crumpled clothes.

Lily passed me a segment of her orange. I ate it but hardly turned my gaze away from the sky. She shuffled around so that she was sitting next to me.

'It's beautiful.'

I nodded.

'You really love Japan, don't you?'

'I suppose so. Yes, I do.'

'Do you think you'll be here for ever?'

'I have no idea.' The image of the ghost volcano seemed to shimmer and I blinked several times and finally turned to face Lily. 'I can't imagine leaving now, that's true.'

We ate in silence, sharing rice balls and barley tea.

'Doesn't Teiji like the mountains?'

I smiled. 'I think he does, but he loves Tokyo best.'

I never took Teiji when I went places with friends. I didn't want to share him. I would meet him later, in the darkest parts of the night, on the street by an empty station, or in one of our apartments. To meet him in an open space, in bright lights, was to expose him to the world from which I wanted to keep him secret.

Perhaps it was strange to Lily that I spent time without him, for her next question was, 'Are you close?'

'We are. Very close.'

'But you don't do everything together. That's nice. You're lucky, Lucy.'

Am I?

*

The descent was fast. We slipped and slid down the paths, tripping sometimes on rocks and roots. I let my feet go too fast and caught my ankle on a tree stump. I flew off the path and landed on my side with my ankle folded under my thigh. I tried to stand but the pain made me dizzy. I sat back down again, bit my lip in some intuitive attempt to move the pain to another place.

Lily rushed to my side. 'OK. Let me check it. Pull your trouser leg up, and your sock down. That's it.'

She loosened my shoe and took my foot in her hands. She prodded firmly but without hurting me.

'It's not broken. It's a nasty sprain, though. Let me get a bandage on it.'

The rest of the group stood around and watched. Bob put one hand on my shoulder and squeezed.

'It's not that bad. It'll be fine.'

'I know. I didn't say it was bad.'

Bob and Natsuko exchanged amused glances. I realized how defensive I'd sounded. Lily gave me a painkiller from a little bag in her rucksack, and some water. After a few minutes' rest I was ready to hop slowly. I felt better. The pain was still sharp but Lily's comforting treatment had touched something deeper in Lucy. All the way down the mountain she glowed in the warmth of Lily's hands on her ankle, of lying on the soil being bandaged and cured. What had touched her most of all was Lily's voice, so unusually calm and competent. Where had that voice come from? Lucy had heard it before in another place.

'You're very good in a crisis, Lily. Did you do Girl Scout training or something?' Bob was also impressed.

'No, no. It's just because I'm a nurse.'

'A nurse? You never told us that.'

Bob was surprised but I knew, as soon as Lily said it, that it made perfect sense.

'Didn't I? It wasn't meant to be a secret. Now I'm working in a bar the topic of nursing doesn't come up very much.'

'I'm glad you were here,' I said, truthfully. 'Not that it's so bad.'

At the bottom Natsuko guided us along small roads to a main one and then to an onsen, a hot spring. After a stretching hike there is nothing better than soaking in the rich minerals of the mountains. We separated, men and women. I entered the changing room with Lily and Natsuko.

Lily was uncomfortable stripping off in front of

other women but did it because she was more embarrassed about being different and making a fuss. I thought her qualms were unnecessary. Lily had a nice body, delicate and slender, while Lucy is built like a crashed tank. Lucy didn't mind communal bathing at all. Once she was in the protection of the hot water, she enjoyed the fact that she could take up more space than the other women. Her body had a greater surface area and therefore she must be deriving more pleasure from the piping water on her skin.

We sat, three in a row, at the taps for the pre-bathing ritual. We showered while sitting on small wooden stools, and filled bowls of water to splosh over our skin. Lily watched Natsuko and me, to make sure she did everything the same way. Once we had washed, I turned the cold tap on full and blasted my ankle for a few moments until it was almost numb.

There were three baths. One was indoors and already full. Women lay stretched out, eyes closed, hair kept off the face by small yellow towels. We went outside where the two baths were almost empty. Water ran from one into the other. A hill rose sharply behind and a thin waterfall slipped over the edge, fell into a stream near the baths. From every direction was the sound of water.

Natsuko went straight for the hottest bath and sat with a small towel over her face. Lily followed but yelped at the heat and jumped out. Her legs were pink from the knees down.

'Don't you like it?' Natsuko asked lazily from under her wet towel.

'I like the idea of it.' Lily hovered, not sure what to do. 'It's just a bit hot.'

'I love it. If I ever have a house of my own, I'd want a natural hot spring in the garden. I'd be happy for ever then.' Natsuko sighed.

'Perhaps this one is a better temperature,' I suggested and went into the other. It was, slightly, and Lily entered the bath with me, carefully and tentatively, limb by limb until just her head stuck out.

The cool air of the late afternoon was as refreshing as the water we bathed in and I closed my eyes to feel it more acutely and to listen to the different sounds of water. I lifted my injured ankle to rest it on the bath's edge. Of course, in a couple of seconds I was thinking of Teiji and how I wished he was in the bath with me, no one else around.

Teiji didn't care about my appearance. I sometimes wondered if he even knew what I looked like. When he stared at me he seemed to be looking beneath the surface of my skin, but I didn't know what he could see. I didn't mind. As long as I kept his attention in this way, I felt lucky. Before my fantasy could get further than Teiji ducking under water to find my legs with his lips, Lily started talking again.

'I wonder what Andy would make of this.'

'He might like it.'

'Doubt it. He doesn't much like things he doesn't know. I'm beginning to think that I only really like things I don't know. Funny that. It never occurred to me we were so diferent. Now it seems obvious. I wish I was like you.'

I was amazed and looked at her, probably suspiciously. Her face was pink under her dyed red hair. She looked uncomfortable in the heat of the bath.

'No, I do. You've got it all together. You're so brainy too. Do you think you and Teiji'll get married?'

'I don't think so.' And with no warning my eyes filled with tears. I splashed them slightly to give myself a reason to wipe my face before Lily noticed.

'Why not?'

I massaged my ankle. The pain was beginning to subside.

'It's not that kind of relationship.'

And immediately I regretted saying it. I didn't know what kind of relationship it was. I'd never thought of it before. Now I had given Lily fuel for another round of questioning.

'Anyway, I'm fine.'

'Is it not a long-term thing, then?'

'It might be but I just haven't thought about it like that. I mean, we don't discuss it because we already have what we want.'

'I'd love to meet him.'

Perhaps she should. Then I could show Teiji that I had friends, too. I was not so obsessed with him that I had to break into his flat when he was out and rifle through his most personal possessions. That was just something that happened, a one-off, a whim. I told Lily none of this. I had a feeling that simply by lying there in the steam, running the thoughts through my mind, Lily might understand them. She leaned over and pressed my ankle between her fingers.

'How does it feel?'

'Fine. Just twingeing a bit.'

'You want to rest it this evening. Get a compress on it and put your feet up.'

'Sounds good. Did you always want to be a nurse?'

'Yes, always. I never thought of anything else.'

'Now you work in a bar. Do you miss nursing?'

'Strangely, no. But I still am a nurse and I'll go back to it. I don't stop feeling like a nurse just because I'm not working as one. You know, I am a nurse. It's what I'll always be.'

'Looking after people, picking up the pieces.'

'Yes.' She smiled and splashed water over her arms. 'Don't you feel that way about translating?'

'The opposite. Even though I work as a translator, I don't feel like one. I don't think of myself as a translator. Perhaps because I don't feel as if I speak two languages any more. It's like one big one with different aspects.'

'The only Japanese I know is what you taught me. Do you speak English or Japanese with Teiji?'

'Both. Either.'

'Are you seeing him tonight?'

'We didn't talk about it. I'll be too tired, anyway.

I may go to see him at the noodle shop tomorrow, though. Yes, I think I'll do that.'

'You told me you'd teach me the words for different kinds of noodles.'

'Did I?'

I knew she was hinting but I hoped she'd take my own hint and give up. She didn't.

'I've hardly eaten any proper Japanese food. I usually go to McDonald's. It's not that I don't want to try Japanese, it's just that I don't know what to ask for, or how to eat it. It would be useful to know.'

I pulled myself out of the water and put my swollen ankle tentatively on the ground. It felt much better.

'All right. If you want to come, I'll be going at about twelve.'

'Shall I come round to your flat? If you tell me where it is—'

'There's no point. It's at the other side of Tokyo from the noodle place. I'll meet you at Takadano-baba station.'

Lily stared at me, appalled that a word could be both so foreign and so long.

'I'll write it down for you,' I said, and went back into the building to find a towel.

Five

I crack my fingers, one by one. Kameyama is tired
of waiting, leans back in his chair with a grunt. I
don't blame him. I can appreciate the annoyance
I am causing. If only I would take some notice of
him, he might make some progress in this case.
But I'm not in the mood to talk, not yet. The thing
is, I don't know what happened that night. It's
a blur in my memory. I have to bring it back,
remember a bit at a time, before I can tell him. Mr
Kameyama will have to be patient. Oguchi is now
playing with the other trouser knee, rubbing it
softly, picking the edge of the seam. His glance
meets mine and he looks away. I think the horror
of the crime that I may have committed is sinking
in. I fix my eyes upon his. His face colours and he
searches for a question with which to break the
silence, which I will not answer.

Kameyama speaks. 'Fine. Let's try another question.'

Yes, let's. Which question shall we try? What's my favourite colour? I don't have one. Do I prefer cats or dogs? Cats, of course; I'm a Leo. How many brothers and sisters do I have? It depends on how you count, whom you count. Have I ever killed anyone? Yes, I have. There was Noah. And while we're talking of death, perhaps this would be a good time to recall the wonderful Mrs Yamamoto, and my days with the magical string quartet which was so important when I first came to Tokyo. Mrs Yamamoto, who died.

'Do you have any hobbies?' Oguchi colours as he asks me this feeble question. Kameyama expels air through his mouth in something between a sigh and a hiss.

'No, I don't.'

And I go back inside my head. But his timing is perfect. It was my search for a hobby that led me to Mrs Yamamoto's door. Since meeting Teiji I'd had no need for hobbies. There was no sense in practising ikebana when I could be having sex, or watching him from behind a book as he served noodles. But when I first arrived in Japan, I knew no one. I was glad to meet people through a shared, civilized interest. It was my participation in Mrs Yamamoto's string quartet that welcomed me to Tokyo, left me certain that this was my home, though it also left me with another corpse on my hands. Clumsy old Lucy.

I told Teiji of my hobby the same night I told him of my childhood – of Lizzie, Noah, and the Rosetta Stone – while he slept like a baby. I held him and continued with my story because it had proved a soothing rock-a-bye. I didn't want him to awaken yet, not while he was so fragile in my arms. I have never held a real baby, but that night I could imagine how it might feel. A calming of the heart-beat, a warmth that I knew would stay in my arms long after he had woken and gone. I kept him there, rocked him, and I told him just a little more, the in-between verses, the adventures I had in Tokyo before I found him by the puddle in Shinjuku.

Not long after arriving in Tokyo, I was given a secondhand cello. I had mentioned my cello-playing past to a high-school girl I taught privately. Two weeks later the student's mother presented me with her old cello saying that they had no space to keep it any more. I was touched but a little nervous. I hadn't played for years and felt a certain responsibility in having my own cello suddenly. I played in my flat for some weeks but found myself at war with my uncultured neighbour. Had she just complained it would have been simple; I would have ignored her and continued to play. Unfortunately she did not opt for the mature response. She switched on her vacuum cleaner every time I started my practice. She opened the windows and doors of her apartment and drowned the voice of my cello's strings. I can only assume she was angry because the infernal noise of my cello prevented her from the pleasure of hearing the cars screeching on and off the tarmac below. I gave up.

But the music had got into my head and wouldn't go away. At work I hummed the pieces I'd played long ago at school. I could remember them note for note, not the melodies, though, just the cello part. I suppose it didn't sound impressive. My Western colleagues complained and glared as I hummed and whistled at my desk, opened and shut the photocopier in time with my droning. I knew it was annoying – Lucy would have glowered at anyone behaving in that manner – but I couldn't stop.

Natsuko said to me one day, 'I think you like music.'

'I think everybody likes music. But I was in the middle of learning something on the cello and now I can't play any more.'

Natsuko told me about Mrs Yamamoto, her old calligraphy teacher, who played the violin with a couple of friends. Mrs Ide played second violin and Mrs Katoh the viola. They had been together for several years but their previous cellist died of a brain tumour. They never gave concerts. Natsuko said they were good but not so brilliant as to be intimidating. At first I wasn't sure they would want me. I am at least twenty years younger than the youngest, Mrs Ide. My conversational Japanese was still not so hot. I could translate the works of Mishima and Tanizaki with relative ease but sometimes found it hard to buy a stamp in a post office. And, of course, I was worried that I would never be a replacement for my predecessor. They told Natsuko they would be pleased to have a cellist in the group. I said to her that I didn't think it was practical to carry a cello from one side of Tokyo to the other every week. Natsuko reported back that Mrs Yamamoto would let me keep the cello in her spare bedroom.

I lugged the cello to the station and took the Yamanote line from Gotanda to Nippori. I entered an
older, quieter part of Tokyo. There were small,
rickety houses here, a few old wooden temples,
stoic survivors of the Great Kanto Earthquake and
the firebombing of World War Two. I stopped in
the Yanaka Cemetery to consult my map and to
have a short rest.

It is a beautiful cemetery, a place to lift your
heart and make you sing. I began to hum 'When
the Saints Go Marching In'. Tombs spread in each
direction, grey geometric shapes ordered into rows
by narrow paths. There were obelisks, stone lanterns, flat headstones. Cherry trees and occasional
pines flanked the paths. Some of the tomb plots
were spacious, considering the size of rooms
alloted to the living in parts of Tokyo. There were
graves in elaborate stone enclosures, raised above
the ground with one or two steps leading up. I
found one that I particularly liked, leaned the cello
against a stone lantern and sat on the step. I was
touched to see that in front of the tall headstone
some devoted person had left two pretty vases
containing purple and white orchids. I tried to read
the characters of the deceased person's name, but
they were too obscure for my Japanese. I looked

around. I could see one or two people dotted in the distance. I thought how nice it would be to be buried here – so peaceful yet still an organic part of the city – and to have my bones and ashes tended to by these kind people.

Natsuko once told me of her grandfather's cremation. Grandpa slid into the oven like a pizza on a tray. When he came out, minus his flesh, his bones were dismantled and presented to the relatives. The guests took long chopsticks and placed the bones into two urns, one for the temple and one for the earth. Grandfather's most special bone was his nodobotoke, his Adam's apple. As it was Buddha-shaped, it had to go into the smaller urn to be preserved at his temple. At the end, the ashes and bits of bone remaining were swept up by a crematorium employee with a small dustpan and brush. That was the part that upset Natsuko. Her grandfather in a dustpan and brush.

Lucy would have no objection to being cremated and demolished by her friends but would not want her remains to be confined to an urn. She would rather be placed directly in the earth, no coffin, no body bag, to come alive again in wriggling worms and grubs. But we don't always get to choose.

A small but sharp breeze stung my lips and made

my eyes water. I looked at the sky. Crows flew overhead, circling and crying like bad omens. One flew down and settled beside me with a piece of white card in its beak. For a moment I thought that it was bearing a message, but it took no notice of Lucy Fly and proceeded to peck and shred the paper. I realized it was part of a cigarette packet and felt foolish. The bird's black eye gleamed in every direction but it had no interest in me. Once it had extracted the silver paper from inside, it discarded the flattened box and flew up into the sky. I lost sight of it among the others.

I didn't want to be late for my first rehearsal so I grabbed the cello by its neck once again and set off into the narrow streets. I followed the efficient directions that Natsuko had written for me and soon found the place. I opened the gate to a two-storey house with a small mossy garden. The front of the house was covered in wisteria. Its leaves trailed over the door frame. I pushed them aside to find the doorbell, excited to be entering a proper house. For months I had been only in flats and offices, and I longed for the cosy domesticity of a real home.

Mrs Yamamoto opened her door to me and

beamed in the porch. She had short silver hair and small round glasses. She was tall and slim.

'*O jama shimasu*,' I said. *I am disturbing you.* I slipped off my shoes and followed her into the tatami room.

Two middle-aged women knelt at the far side of the low table. The sun shone through the paper doors behind them. The woman to the left spoke first. She was stocky with a round face and pudding-bowl haircut.

'*Konnichiwa. Ide to moushimasu.*' She smiled broadly.

'*Hajimemashite*,' I said, tipping my head slightly. The other woman smiled nervously and bowed.

'*Katoh desu. Yoroshiku onegai shimasu.*'

She was small with frizzy grey hair and birdlike features. Her eyes darted quickly between the three of us and later I learned that this was natural to her. She could not rest her eyes upon a person or object for more than a few seconds but she had a nervous giggle that followed every utterance and gesture, except when she was playing her viola.

'Lucy *desu*,' I said. 'Lucy Fly. Fly Lucy. *Yoroshiku onegai shimasu.*'

I knelt on the tatami. It was soft and had a summery smell of grass and dust.

Mrs Yamamoto served us green tea and pink bean-paste cakes from a lacquer tray. We sat silently as the cups and teapot clinked, tea poured into the cups. The silence was, for me, a good sign. I looked forward to the pleasure of being with people without the strain of perpetual talking and listening.

I had not been in Japan long enough to appreciate the bitter taste of the tea and the sickly sweetness of the bean paste. That first day each mouthful was an effort. But over the following weeks I began to associate the sweet-bitter taste with pure, silent enjoyment. Somehow the smell of the tatami and the resin for our bows became part of that taste and I can still find it on my tongue. I grew accustomed to slicing through the soft cake with my shard of wood, eating it in slivers between sips of hot tea, looking forward to hours of shared music.

The first Sunday I was surprised when Mrs Ide and Mrs Katoh drank up their tea and then began to scrutinize the cups. I realized that it was polite to do so and copied them. The cups were all different. Mrs Yamamoto had a collection. When I held my cup to the light, gold flecks glittered and made me smile. I didn't want to put the cup down again. Of course I did, because Miriam's reedy voice resonated in the room. 'People don't buy cups to have them picked up and gawped at. You'll have it in pieces.'

That morning, between silences, we talked about the consistency of the tea, the differences between making Japanese tea and English tea (green tea is best made with water at a temperature of eighty to ninety degrees, never boiling). We discussed the cake, the wagashi. The soft, sticky bun was wrapped in a leaf. I didn't know what tree it was picked from but it tasted sharp and sweet.

Mrs Yamamoto whisked away our cups and plates and invited us through to her Western-style living room. I was a little disappointed to leave the peace of the tatami room, but for our musical purposes I could see that we needed to be on chairs.

Mrs Yamamoto set up the music stands. She led us through some scales and basic studies to warm up. When her bow touched the strings we followed obediently. I was out of practice and missed a few sharps and flats, but no one commented. When we were ready to play music, my mind was clear and focused.

Mrs Yamamoto passed around the music and we spent the morning playing Haydn. We stopped whenever Mrs Yamamoto frowned and we played sections or phrases repeatedly until between us we found their meaning. We hardly spoke. The music pulled us together. Though I'd played in the orchestra at school and had been told many times to listen to the other players, this was the first time that I had ever felt compelled to do so. When Lizzie the trombonist was my musical partner, I had to concentrate hard on not listening to her because she was so loud. I got into the habit of playing with my ear almost touching the strings so I could be sure I was hitting the right notes. This was different.

Inside the music, I was comfortably alone with my own thoughts. I had a burst of optimism about Japan. Of course I knew I would be here a long time – I had known that before I came – but for the first time I felt a kind of thrill. What would I do here? What kind of person could Lucy become, so far away from home?

We stopped briefly for lunch and then moved on to Mozart and played until sunset. There were wrong notes, unarticulated sections, shaky rhythms. We were not professionals but the way the three women played together was beautiful. Though it took me time to locate my own place in the group, their support was like the thick hot water of an onsen. By the time we put down our bows and folded the music stands, I didn't need to be told that I was a full quarter of the whole.

Mrs Yamamoto's teenage daughter brought coffee and then they told me their stories. Mrs Ide – the pudding bowl – was born in Manchuria, just before the Pacific War. She remembered nothing of the war itself but immediately afterwards her family had to return to Japan. They walked at night, hundreds of miles to the coast. There was no map or compass but in the darkness they followed the stars until they reached the coast of the Yellow Sea. Mrs Ide's younger sister never made it. She disappeared along the way and Mrs Ide was never told where she went or why.

Mrs Katoh was from Sado Island in the Sea of Japan. All she told me was that she had left her husband and son a few years before and come to live in Tokyo, alone.

'I exiled myself,' she said. 'I'll never go back there. Throughout history people were sent to

Sado Island as exiles, but I did it the other way round. You should go there if you have the opportunity, though. It's Japan's secret jewel. People forget it's there, poked up there in the sea, but it's beautiful.' She giggled.

I wondered what had happened to make her leave Sado, but I never found out.

For several years I played my cello with the threesome almost every Sunday. It was the high point of my week and I started looking forward to it on Wednesday or Thursday. I never thought those days would end but they did.

One Sunday the telephone rang as I was about to leave my flat. It was Mrs Katoh. There would be no practice that day. Her voice was deeper, flatter than usual and she didn't giggle. There would be no practice again. Mrs Yamamoto had met with an accident. She had gone upstairs that morning to dust the spare bedroom. She didn't know that Lucy had set a deadly trap in there, but neither did Lucy. Normally, after a session, I lugged my cello up to the spare room and left it next to the wardrobe. The last time, for a reason I still cannot fathom, I'd rested it behind the bed, a little out of the way. Evidently, Mrs Yamamoto hadn't noticed, and while she was dusting the cupboards she tripped backwards over my instrument and hit her head on the floor. When her husband found her, she was no longer breathing.

I didn't want to play the cello again. I didn't want to meet Mrs Ide and Mrs Katoh any more. I didn't contact them, nor did I ever ask about reclaiming the cello from the Yamamotos' spare room. Her death had upset me more than I could have imagined, as if I'd lost a lifelong friend. There were aspects of those days, though, that I wanted to keep in my life.

A couple of months after Mrs Yamamoto's death, I joined a tea ceremony class. Of course, I was hoping to find again the simple pleasure of the teacup, the sweet cake, the tatami and the beautiful quiet touched only by the clink of the teapot. But the other women in the group were not so serious. They gossiped and chattered throughout the proceedings. They couldn't remember one part of the ceremony correctly from week to week because they were never listening properly the first time. I found no depth of concentration. Nor was the gossip particularly interesting, and so I gave up.

There was just one thing from the string quartet

that I kept and followed through. It was Sado Island. Mrs Katoh had told me many times of this beautiful, remote place and I thought about it often. I planned to visit one day but in all my plans I was there alone. In fact, when I finally went, it was with Lily and Teiji as my travelling companions. It is sad but I cannot thank Mrs Katoh for Sado Island – look where it has got me.

But there was much time between to be filled in and after Mrs Yamamoto's death, I took to wandering around Tokyo alone. I had friends at work – Japanese and non-Japanese – but I avoided going out with them more than once or twice a month. I couldn't bear to spend my life talking to people. It seemed wasteful.

I used to take the Yamanote line to any station, then follow the tracks to the next one, or further. That was how I came to be in Shinjuku the night I met Teiji. I would not have said that I was lonely in those days – I never felt lonely – and yet when I saw Teiji there, silent and studious, I could not bear to walk away from him and be alone again.

We had silent conversations with invisible gestures. We walked around the streets together. We hung out in his uncle's noodle shop. While Teiji was serving customers or taking out the rubbish, I read the novels of Mishima and Soseki Natsume, *The Tale of Genji*. Where the Japanese was too difficult, I used a translated text to help me. I wrote new kanji in a notebook, practised the form until I knew the stroke order as well as I knew how to write Lucy Fly.

We spent whole weekends in bed. But our favourite thing was to go out in the rain on a warm night. And here are conversations I know we had. Teiji taught me the Japanese adverbs to describe different types of rainfall, the kinds of words that don't always show up in a Japanese –English dictionary. *Potsu potsu* is fine, spitting rain. *Zaa zaa* is a downpour. In my memories of the time I spent with Teiji, it always seems to be the rainy season.

The nights have become jumbled in my mind and maybe I am confusing them, but what I remember is this.

I am lying on the floor looking up at Teiji's ceiling. Teiji slips into the room and grabs my hand.

'It's raining. We can't stay indoors. Come on.'

He pulls me out into the street. I am laughing (I *am*). He is wearing cut-off jeans and flip-flops.

I can't picture my own clothes but I know my feet are bare. We splash through puddles and follow the shiny pavements from one road to the next. On the main highway car tyres screech, crowds push forward with umbrellas. On a smaller street we can hear each raindrop land in its destination, a leaf, a windowsill, a flower petal, *potsu potsu*.

We race each other, kicking up dirty water, to the railway bridge. In the shelter of the Yamanote and Chuo lines, we lean against the concrete wall and wait for a train to pass over our heads. Since the Yamanote trains go at intervals of three minutes or so, we don't need to be patient. I kiss Teiji, holding him so tightly that drops of water squeeze from our T-shirts. He touches his nose softly against mine and smiles. I let my tongue touch his teeth, crooked pearls which I love. When the Shibuya-bound train rattles over our heads a thrill runs from the tip of my nose down to the backs of my knees. It is quiet again. Teiji unhooks my bra and slips it out through the sleeve of my T-shirt with a flickering smile. Abracadabra. His forehead pushes my T-shirt higher so his hair is brushing my skin. He kisses my nipples with rainy lips and when the next trainful of commuters runs over our heads, we are fucking. The rough concrete wall makes pink and white lines on my back and tugs hard at the ends of my hair.

Recently, I have tortured myself by standing under railway bridges, making myself shiver when a train passes. Then I weep because Teiji's smile and Teiji's body are not there and because I'm so stupid. Then I cry more because my sobs are echoing and returning to me, showing me how foolish I am. And I cry for Lily too.

'No hobbies at all?' Oguchi gives me a look which is almost a cry.

'None. I don't need hobbies. That doesn't make me a murderer, though.'

He is flustered, clears his throat, says nothing.

They stand up together and leave the room. I am promised that they will be back later, with reinforcements, to get some sense out of me. When the door is safely locked behind them, I sink from my chair to the floor, crawl to the corner of the room and crouch against the wall. Then I cry for Lily.

Six

Sachi was in the middle of the photograph box and Lucy was at the top. I knew my place and it was a better one than hers. It was the best position of all. I didn't consider myself jealous, not in the sense that I thought Teiji still loved Sachi. But I couldn't get rid of her. I was terrified of the day that my photographs would be replaced by a layer of new ones, of the next person or object. I imagined myself spinning off into darkness, nothingness, like Sachi. I wondered what had become of her, what was the point of those bleak parties where she came to look unhappier, sicker. I wrote many stories in my head and soon began to think of her as someone I had always known, a sister even.

The story told by Teiji's photographs was this. There was a young man who sometimes came into the noodle shop for a cheap meal before going to some small theatre. He loved plays and dance so much that he couldn't bear to spend his evenings anywhere else. He went as often as he could afford tickets and to all kinds of shows. The theatre made him weep. At the sight of the actors or dancers entering the lights as the play started, his tear ducts moistened and his nose stung. Best of all were the white-faced dancers of butoh. Their gestures, aggressive and erotic, touched him deep inside, set his legs quivering. He liked musicals too – whether danced, rollerskated, or performed on ice – and the happier the songs, the harder he cried. He could soak three or four handkerchiefs in an evening watching the spectacular song and dance numbers of the all-female Takarazuka.

When Teiji saw him in the restaurant, the crying man was always nervous, a little tense, like someone killing time before an interview or exam. He would tell Teiji of the play he was to see and sometimes, choked with sobs, talked of the previous night's theatrical adventure.

Teiji took a few photographs of this man, but couldn't be satisfied. The crying man looked rigid and ordinary, even when red-eyed. He allowed Teiji to take the pictures but said, 'You don't want to take photographs of me. You should go to the theatre. There's nothing interesting about my life. I'm the audience. Nothing's ever happened to me, or ever will. That's why I go to watch. It's not that I dream of being an actor, you see. That's a mistake a lot of people make. My role is to be in the audience and my duty is to do it well. I want to be watching the performers. There *is* nothing for you to photograph.'

Teiji became curious about the theatre, this part of the city he had never met. He went to a little-known venue one night to see a play. He thought there would be new images to photograph and so there were. The play was a one-woman show starring a student actress. When she stepped out onto the lonely stage in her brown military uniform that he didn't recognize from any army, Teiji knew that he needed to catch her in his camera. Her face was young and a little soft but she shouted with the aggression and ugliness of a middle-aged man. From the back of the audience Teiji took her picture, just one. When the play was almost over he slipped out to wait for her beside the stage door. She was alone. He looked at her through the lens and when she saw him she smiled. To be photographed by every newspaper and magazine in Japan was her aim. This was a start.

They went to a bar near the theatre and stayed all night.

Off the stage she was sullen and unhappy but glad, at least, to be with Teiji. He didn't require her to perform, even to speak. He was fascinated by what she was, the image she left in his eyes. Sachi trusted him. Then, as she grew weaker, she came to need him.

He went to the theatre between shifts at work. When he couldn't go to performances he settled for rehearsals. In different theatres and different plays he saw her as a princess, a secretary, a concubine. She strutted in a costume made of peacock feathers, danced on her toes in a black leotard. He didn't care much to follow the plots of the dramas and rarely remembered the story. Often he didn't notice that there was a story. He was excited only by the sight of Sachi, her costume, voice and face, the gestures she used. After performances and rehearsals Teiji met her outside the stage door, or in some coffee shop or bar near the theatre. Sachi chain-smoked and they would sit together behind a gauze of cigarette smoke. She laughed and cried alternately, sometimes with a hacking cough. She didn't care for the world of theatre but didn't belong in any other. They went to parties where she drank too much and cried in the bathroom. She didn't like the people and was bad at party small-talk, but couldn't stop herself going. She had to be where the actors and actresses were. Sometimes Teiji learned that after getting her home she'd called a taxi and returned to the party she'd hated so much. He thought she wanted to destroy herself. She stopped going to rehearsals, stopped getting up during the day and soon no director wanted to cast her. She was addicted to the parties she couldn't bear and even Teiji couldn't save her from them.

And there the story was interrupted because Teiji had found me flicking through his pictures. But the final image continued to haunt me. Sachi lying on the pavement. It could have been an overdose, drunkenness, sleep or death. I didn't ask Teiji about Sachi again. And of course, I know nothing of the crying man. I made it up. Perhaps he never went to the theatre in his life. It could have been that his noodles were too hot, and so his eyes were red and moist in the photograph I saw.

I thought of going to the theatre to find Sachi, but how would I know which one? I could scour an entertainment magazine to find out what was on and where, but it was risky. A theatre is a dangerous place for Lucy. I can't watch a play without believing I am in it, or even that I am it. As a child I went on occasional school trips to see Shakespeare, or a pantomime, never anything between. I dreaded the plays in the same way that I sometimes feared sleep. I would be sucked into a nightmare and might never wake up. And yet, once I was there, waiting on my velvet folding seat for the lights to go down, I became involved in the drama with the embracing passion of a schoolgirl. I scarcely breathed until the lights came up, such was my concentration. The concept of invited audience participation has always struck Lucy as bizarre. I *was* participating. I was every character, and the place and plot too. Whether I was Falstaff or a babe in the wood, whether I was a murder or a mystery, I lived it to the full. I was both Titania and Oberon, Demetrius and Lysander, Puck and Flute the bellows-mender. I was Wall and Moonlight. I was also Snow White and all the Seven Dwarves. I was the skull of Yorick and I was a very sharp rapier. When the curtain came down, I couldn't bear to leave and yet I wanted to. A teacher would drag me along the aisle and toward the minibus. I kicked and screamed, lost fingernails and hair to the theatre. It was a kind of madness because it made no difference whether I stayed in the theatre or whether I returned home to my bedroom. I would be stuck inside the play for weeks and months, living it again and again, changing and developing it each day obsessively and against my will. People around me were barely visible, hardly audible. Then, as I emerged from the frenzy, I would enjoy the calm and await the next trip with terror.

I'm not forced to visit theatres any more, so I don't. Such a loss of self-control would be intolerable; I would never be able to concentrate on my translations. No, I couldn't look for Sachi in a theatre. Besides, according to the photographs, she was no longer there. She wasn't anywhere.

I went, after Lily's death, to a pond near my apartment. I looked for Teiji's reflection in the water. I wanted him to teach me words of comfort but I found only turtles and carp. I was drunk. I was off food at the time and so I'd had gin for breakfast. It's a pleasant way to begin the day. Before the glass was empty I felt as if the day had been dealt with, was out of my hands, and I was free to do whatever I liked. I wandered past the reeds and waterlilies, unable to focus my eyes. A profusion of colour – corn-blue sky, green-headed ducks, a scarlet wooden bridge – throbbed hazily. A shrine stood beside the pond and I wondered whether or not it would be all right to clap my hands before it and say a prayer for Lily and Teiji. I decided it was probably best not to pray when drunk, and went to watch the carp swimming.

On a bench in front of me a young man stretched out in the sun. He might have been a runner, for he wore baggy shorts and his top was bare. He had brown skin and long black hair that fell over the end of the bench in a single ponytail. His chest glistened in the light, rising and falling gently as he breathed. The reeds behind him swayed slightly and flies buzzed around. The whole place seemed to breathe with him, as if each breath he took filled the earth's lungs. I stared beyond him, at the water and the wooden shrine but all I saw was that thick black hair, curved eyelids, glinting brown skin.

I sat on the ground, among swollen pink azaleas, and shut my eyes while the earth tilted and swayed like the deck of a ship. I wanted Teiji so badly, to touch his skin, but I would never, ever see him again. When I threw up, a couple of hours later, I blamed it not on alcohol but on seasickness.

Seven

The noodle shop was crowded. As always, most of the customers were men. Businessmen, young and old, students. There were just a few women, sitting in pairs or alone, facing the wall. Through the window I could almost smell the food, the chopped spring onions, the small pieces of meat, the barley tea. I pushed the door open and entered with Lily close behind. The toe of her shoe clipped my heel twice as we walked. I wished she would step out beside me but I knew she liked to hide. She'd done the same thing when we were flat-hunting, pushing me into the firing line and cowering in my shadow. I searched for Teiji's face but could not see him. His uncle nodded at me from behind the counter. It wasn't a look of open hostility but I knew he was suspicious. He always looked straight into my eyes for a couple of seconds then averted his stare to some stain on the floor, or the back of a chair. I thought it was a sad look, but I didn't know why he should be sad. I wondered what he had thought of Sachi, the strange actress.

I said konnichiwa in a cheery voice and led Lily past him to the only empty table. Once we were seated I realized that I had my back to the kitchen. This was no good because I would not be able to look out for Teiji, to thrill at a glimpse of his muscles as he wiped a surface or opened a cupboard before seeing me and coming to join us. I was about to ask Lily to change places but before my mouth was open I sensed Teiji's presence close behind me. It was a kind of warmth, a pull, and I leaned back in my chair to let my head touch his chest, like a magnet snapping onto another. Lily looked up, beyond my head and back at me. I couldn't tell what she thought of him, though she seemed a little shy. She waited for me to speak. Lily was the first friend I'd introduced to Teiji. It gave me an odd feeling of sharing a deeply personal secret. I confess, I wanted her to like him.

'This is Teiji,' I said, still not looking.

''Ello.'

Teiji greeted her, brushed my hair with his

fingertips. He went back into the kitchen, promising to join us in a moment.

'He's very cute,' Lily whispered with an encouraging nod. Cute. It was close to insulting but she intended it as a compliment so I forgave her. I wanted Lily to like Teiji but I had not expected her to understand him. Teiji's world was too distant from hers.

He appeared again with two hot bowls of noodles and placed them on the table. His camera was around his neck, hanging by its old leather strap. I was sure it hadn't been there when he stood behind me. I plucked disposable chopsticks from the pot on the table but Teiji put his hand around mine and steered it back. He disappeared, then came back with lacquer chopsticks that, I guessed, he and his uncle used. Teiji once told me that they ate together most evenings. Sometimes it was midnight before they were both free to sit at the table, but still one would wait for the other, however hungry he felt. Teiji's uncle liked to talk about things he'd noticed during the day, a bird on the windowsill, a customer's gold tooth. Teiji would listen and eat.

'Wow. We're getting the posh treatment.' Lily picked up the chopsticks and peered at them as if

they were made of ivory. I am still finding it difficult to remember Teiji's words and so I will recount
what I believe he may, or must have said that day.

'Enjoy your noodles. I'll come and talk to you
when I can but I have to serve these customers
first.'

Lily poked the noodles around the bowl. She
knew how to hold her chopsticks but not how to
grip slippery food. I was glad because her concentration rendered her silent for at least twenty
minutes and so I was allowed to let my thoughts
wander while I slurped from my own bowl. I
turned every now and then to see what Teiji was
doing. He moved around the shop clearing tables,
wiping them. Although he performed each task
efficiently, his thoughts were clearly elsewhere. His
eyes were full of something that was not tables nor
damp cloths. I hoped it was me but it was hard to
tell. I finished my noodles and watched Lily as she
fought her way toward the bottom of her bowl.
We were startled by a flash and both turned at the
same time. Of course, I should have known by
then. I should have known exactly what it was and
not even blinked.

Teiji had captured us in his lens. Snap. He
smiled, turned and went back to clearing tables.

He had taken a photograph of Lily and me together. He gave it to me a couple of weeks later. He'd wrapped it in a piece of carefully folded newspaper. I kept that too. I read both sides of it again and again to decipher some message of love. On one side was an article about the recent rise in domestic abuse, on the other were that day's foreign exchange rates. I could make a link, if I tried, but I knew none was intended. Still, it had been folded by Teiji's dextrous hands, for me. I was glad that he hadn't made a copy of the photograph for Lily. That meant it that it was intended as a picture of me with Lily as an extra, not a picture of the two of us as equals. I was ashamed of my delight in such a childish triumph, but not enough to make me change that feeling. Nor was my shame sufficient to lead me to the photography shop and have it copied for Lily, though I knew even then that she would have liked it. I still have that picture, in a box where I put things that I don't want to keep but cannot throw away.

It seems to Lucy now that the photograph marks the start of the trouble. I could look at the picture and think, this is the moment where it went wrong, the point at which it was already too late. Before the shutter clicked. After the shutter clicked. A split second in between when a seismic shift occurred that could not be felt on the earth's crust. It would eventually result in an earthquake so huge that it couldn't be measured on either the Richter scale or the Japanese earthquake scale. In fact the photograph shows nothing but Lily and Lucy sitting at a table; it was the taking of the photograph, not the image it stole, that started the rumbling. And I don't have a photograph of the photograph being taken. Yet the picture shows what was happening in the moment it was taken and so it has become a representation of itself. I should have understood this at the time.

But I didn't. My head was full of Sachi.

Other customers came and left, staying just long enough to have their noodles and pay for them. It was a functional place, after all. But Lily wanted to talk and we chatted through the afternoon, mostly about her apartment. She was delighted with her new home and gave me all the credit, as if I'd built it for her with my own hands. She told me of all the little things she'd bought – a mosquito-killing machine, a rice cooker. I listened but I was not enjoying myself in this uncomfortable clashing of my life's zones. I wanted to get Lily out of the shop, but Teiji was there. I couldn't leave him. My fingertips twitched, as they do when I'm annoyed, and I kept them pressed hard against the table leg.

At about five o'clock Teiji finished work and suggested we went for a beer together. I willed Lily to refuse, but knew she wouldn't. Since meeting Lucy she seemed to have no need for other friends.

'I think Lily wants to get back home.'

'No, no. I'd love to go for a drink. Is there a bar near here?'

Teiji nodded. I was irritated but the only way out would be for me to go home alone. I wanted to be with Teiji so I couldn't leave. Teiji seemed happy for Lily to join us. I wondered if he was afraid of being alone with me, scared that I would start to ask about Sachi again.

We walked out into daylight and Teiji led us to an izakaya, a large bar with long low tables and tatami floors. We slipped off our shoes and stepped up into the dark room. Several waiters shouted their welcomes to us and one led us to a corner table. Teiji and I sat at one side, Lily at the other. We ordered large bottles of beer and a bowl of salty green soy beans. When the food and drink arrived, Lily's eyes were shining.

'Have you been out much in Tokyo, Lily?' I asked, knowing that she hadn't.

'Not really. I'm working in the bar almost every afternoon and evening. I don't like to go out with colleagues all the time either so . . . Now I'm living by myself, though, it's a bit lonely sometimes. Not that I don't like my flat or anything, I love it.' She smiled gratefully at me. 'The other people I meet are all teachers, you know. You've met some of them, of course. Bob's nice. I don't think we've got much in common, though. I mean, you're a translator, I know, but you're different. Maybe it's because we come from the same place.'

I explained to Teiji, through a tense jaw, that Lily and I were from the same part of the same county. This seemed to interest him, though he was fast becoming drunk and unfocused, as was Lily. It takes more than a couple of glasses of beer to affect Lucy and so I drank heartily to catch up with them. Teiji said to Lily, 'You don't seem like other foreigners in Japan.'

'What do you mean?'

'I don't know. I think you weren't so ready to come here. Perhaps you were happier at home.'

'I wasn't happy at home, but it's true, I'm different from the other Westerners I meet. They're brainier.'

Neither of us refuted the observation, but Teiji stared at her thoughtfully.

'You were a nurse in Britain? That takes skills not many people have.'

'Perhaps.'

'You must be very patient, and very practical.'

'I do try. I don't always get it right of course. I miss the hospital though, lots.'

'But working in a bar. That's not so bad, is it? I think it's a good kind of work. The noodle shop gives me all the time I need for thinking because my body just gets on with the job by itself.'

'I'm so bad at bar work. I have to concentrate all the time, otherwise I'd be even worse.'

They talked more, but I have no idea where the conversation went next. I was surprised by Teiji. He'd never told me about his love for mopping floors and washing up. We didn't discuss such mundane notions. We talked about typhoons, volcanoes, about the light on a winter morning. Mostly, I think, we didn't talk. And that was my favourite thing. Not talking. Not feeling the need to fill up beautiful and valuable silences with unnecessary noise.

Lily was a chatterbox. I'd wanted her to make me ordinary in front of Teiji – talking about everyday things – so he'd forget my act of treachery. Instead, in taking on Teiji in conversation, she was making him into something ordinary. I didn't like it – for me Teiji was made of magic – so I didn't listen. I settled into thinking about Lily in her white uniform, tending to patients in a hospital ward. She would have seen deadly illnesses, bloody injuries, grief. From nowhere the seven brothers marched into my mind with their fishing nets, and then Noah's final trip to the hospital with his blood-matted curls, though he was almost dead. The doctors and nurses rushed and fought to save his life. They fought with all their might, but they lost. And somewhere from the battlefield a nurse was coming to take Lucy away, a beautiful nurse with crinkly eyes.

'Did you ever have to deal with dead children?' The question slipped out.

Teiji stared at me. He looked as if something had stuck in his throat. Lily was unfazed.

'Yes. Dead everything, really. It's my job. That doesn't make it easy when a kid dies, but—' She sipped her beer and frowned.

'But?'

'I can't remember what I was going to say. This beer's gone right to my head. I'm pissed.'

'Me too.'

If Teiji was alarmed by my question, he soon recovered. He was now laughing. His face was pink from the alcohol. He looked as if he'd been tickled. I had never seen him even slightly tipsy before and I felt confused. He was relaxed and his smile was sweet but it was different from the smile I knew. I touched his cheek with the backs of my fingers. His skin was burning. He took my wrist to keep my hand in place.

'You're very hot, Teiji.'

'Yes. I have too much to drink and then I boil up. I need air to cool me down again. Let's go somewhere else for the next drink. I'd like to sit in the park.'

'Is there a park near here?' Lily practically squealed.

'Not especially near,' Teiji replied, 'but it's nice outside. We can walk.'

Night had fallen while we were in the bar. In Yoyogi Park we sat on plastic bags from a convenience store and stacked cans of beer around us. We opened packets of small rice crackers with tiny dried fish and spread them on the grass. The lights from the city twinkled through the high trees. Lily watched and began to sing.

'*Sometimes I walk away, when all I really wanna do—*'

'You've got a nice voice.' My compliment was genuine. Her singing voice was rich and pure, without a trace of the whine she used when she spoke.

'Thanks – *is love and hold you right. There is just one thing I can say . . .*'

'This is a perfect summer evening.' I lay back on the grass and let the insects feed on my blood.

'*It's all right. Can't you see – the downtown lights.*'

'Downtown lights,' Teiji murmured. 'In every city in the world. I'd like to see London's downtown lights.'

Lily piped up, 'So would I. I've only been to London twice and both times I was there in the daytime. But I've never seen city lights like Tokyo's before. So big and so bright. All those big words everywhere, flashing on and off. What I like best is when city lights are shining on water, you know, when it's raining, or if there's a river in the city. I love that.'

Teiji put his arm round me and with his other hand reached for a beer and snapped it open, handed it to me, kissed the side of my neck. I thought of Sachi's neck, long and soft.

'Singing is good,' Teiji announced. 'It's like breathing from a deep place, not your lungs but your spirit. I don't know any English songs, though, except the Beatles and I haven't learned the words to those.'

I'd never heard him sing before, nor say that he wanted to. But then, I'd never heard his speech slur with drunkenness before, either.

'Teach me a Japanese song.' Lily was standing now, swaying a little as she sipped from her can. 'I want to learn a Japanese song.'

Teiji closed his eyes and I thought he was drifting off into his own world. After a few seconds he opened them, smiled at Lily.

'All right. I'll teach you an easy one. Everyone in Japan knows this song.'

And, slowly, the three of us sang '*Ue o Muite Arukou*' together. Lily couldn't grasp the words but sang loudly with meaningless approximations and didn't listen when I tried to translate the meaning for her.

Ue o muite

Arukou . . .
'Walk with your face upward,' I chipped in.
Namida ga koborenai you ni . . .
'So as not to let the tears fall . . .'
Omoidasu, haru no hi . . .
Hitori botchi no yoru.
'When, on a lonely evening, you are reminded of a spring day.' I repeated the last line in my head. 'Or is it the other way round? It's difficult to translate.'

Lily didn't mind what the lyrics were, but she sang several times.

'I'm really too drunk.' Teiji opened another can of beer and started the next verse of the song.

'Let's walk around. The night is beautiful.' Lily spun on her heels and giggled.

We collected our things and began to walk. As we stood I noticed that Teiji had left his camera on the ground. He never forgot his camera. I picked it up and slung it round my neck. I would produce it when he noticed it was missing. Lily started to sing again and Teiji tried to correct her mistakes.

Behind them, I slipped the lens cap off the camera, raised the camera to my eye and, though it was harder to focus my own eyes than it was to focus the lens, I managed to catch them both in the square of the viewfinder. The flash was bright but they continued walking and singing as if they'd noticed nothing. I put the camera away and chased after Teiji. Suddenly it seemed vital that I return it to him.

Now I have changed my mind and I see that it was probably this photograph in Yoyogi Park, rather than the one in the noodle shop, that was my downfall. Or else Lucy is too superstitious, looking for clues in everything when in fact there are none in anything.

In the early hours of the morning we were walking the streets, following a road uphill toward Teiji's flat. Lily kept falling to the ground and saying she would sleep on the pavement and we were not to worry. Each time, we picked her up between us and hauled her a few steps further. Lily was not heavy but alcohol had depleted Teiji's usual strength and coordination. He kept walking into me and I found I was doing most of the work. Teiji spotted a small trolley at the side of the road, the kind used for moving boxes around a warehouse or unloading goods from a van. He motioned for me to follow him. We lifted Lily onto it and pushed her further up the road. Her head rolled backward and her red tuft of hair hung over the side of the platform. Her legs and arms seemed to fall in every direction. She looked like a crushed spider. The sky was the prickly darkness of early morning just before dawn.

Five minutes later Lily was walking again and I was lying on the trolley. By the time we reached the top of the street, the sky was lighter and now I was pushing the trolley with Teiji and Lily squashed on it together. I stopped to rest and enjoy the view. Ahead of me, between the buildings on the almost empty road, the sun hung in the sky, a huge pink ball, swelling and glowing before my eyes. I pushed the trolley to an alley that ran between two shops, wedged it against a wall so it couldn't slide around, and collapsed on top of Lily and Teiji. My head was full of the noise of our voices singing in the park, and the dawn chorus.

How could I have known, in the midst of that cacophony, the size of the silence that would soon fall upon Tokyo, upon Lily, Teiji, and Lucy?

Eight

A week or two after our night in the park, Lily came to visit. It was late and I wasn't expecting her but I recognized her finger on my doorbell in the same way that I knew Teiji's. Teiji's ring was soft but even. Lily pressed too hard and too long, a statement of nervousness, a lack of self-control.

I opened the door. She'd been crying.

'Come in. What's wrong?'

'I'm not disturbing you, am I? I don't want to get in your way if Teiji's here.'

'He isn't. He's working late tonight. The restaurant's busy.'

'Oh, right.'

She followed me into my main room, hovered in the middle.

'Sit down.'

'Ta. I'm really sorry about this. I don't know why I didn't phone first. I just got up and came out. I didn't know who else to go to. This is a lovely flat. Nice and uncluttered.'

'Bare. It's the way I like it.' I wished she would get to the point. What was she doing in my flat so late at night?

'You don't have photos of your family anywhere?'

'None.'

'What about Teiji's photos? Don't you like to put them on the walls?'

'I keep them in a drawer. A couple I use as bookmarks or whatever. I write shopping lists on the backs of some, but I don't throw them away afterwards.'

'Why do you scribble on the back of a perfectly nice photograph? I'll buy you a notebook if you're short of paper.'

'No, no. Thanks. I like things around me to be useful. Otherwise, why would I keep them?'

It was not a truthful answer, but Lily wouldn't have understood the truth. I kept Teiji's pictures in a drawer that I opened every night and every morning. Seeing myself through his eyes was the best way to see him when he wasn't with me. I made notes on the backs of his photographs because sometimes I didn't feel like writing on anything that wasn't his.

I sat on the floor, waited for Lily to explain herself. She said nothing, walked to the window and stuck her head out.

'Noisy with the windows open.'

'Yes, but it's too hot otherwise.'

'How do you manage without air-conditioning?'

'I sweat a lot.'

She sat on a cushion, curled her legs beside her, leaned against the wall.

'I feel strange.'

'Has something happened?'

'Yes, well. Yes it has and no it hasn't.'

'You mean?'

'I had a letter from Andy. He wants me to go back.'

'He's got your address? I thought you'd kept it top secret.'

'No, he hasn't got it. He sent a letter to my friend and she's forwarded it to me. The thing is that she's the one I stayed with before I came out to Japan. She helped me get the job and everything. That means that he's traced me to her at least. The next step will be to find out I'm in Tokyo. There are people in the pubs near her house who could tell him that much.'

'Yes, but even if he discovers you're here, how on earth would he find your tiny flat in Tokyo?'

'I know you're right but it just frightened me when I got the letter. I feel stupid panicking about it. The truth is, I was just starting to feel good without him. I'm getting used to working here and living here. I'd almost forgotten all about England. It was quite nice, actually. And now here he bloody is again.'

'Is he really that bad? What are you so frightened of? You've left the country – surely that's evidence enough that you've left him too.'

Lily said nothing. She shook her head.

'Is he violent?'

'Not with me. Only with men he thinks are talking to me too much, or looking at me. I mean, what a joke. Who'd be looking at me?'

Anyone would rather look at Lily's pretty face than at Lucy, but I didn't want to point this out while she was feeling so sorry for herself with such success.

'Even if he did get your address, would he seriously come all the way to Japan? It's a long

way to travel just to be dumped by a woman who's
already left you.'

'If he's got the money, he'll come. That's a big
if, mind you.'

'So tell him to get lost, get back on his plane.'

She laughed, picked at her cuticles. 'You know
what he did once? It's embarrassing. He wanted to
hire a private detective to snoop on me but he
couldn't afford it. So instead he bought a cheap
bugging device from some dodgy bloke in a pub
and put it in the lining of my handbag.'

'He spied on you?'

'Yes, but I spotted it straight away. He'd ripped
the lining to put the thing in and then tried to sew
it up again, but made a right pig's ear. I found it
when I was hanging my bag in my locker at work.
I didn't know what it was for weeks, mind you,
and I didn't like to ask. I just put it on the shelf in
my locker and forgot about it. I suppose the only
thing he picked up was the door opening and
closing and the sound of the key in the lock.'

'So how did you find out what it was?'

'I caught him going through my bag a couple of
times. In the end it dawned on me what he was
looking for. I showed it to someone at work and
they told me what it was. I chucked it away, not

before toying with the idea of attaching it to an ambulance siren, mind you, give the bugger something to listen to.'

I looked at her.

'I know what that look means. Why didn't I leave him sooner?'

'Well, why?'

'Because I knew he'd follow me and then I'd have to deal with the rows and everything. It was just less hassle to stay with him until I could get so far away he wouldn't find me.'

'Logical.'

'I know, I know. If I was you I'd just have said get lost and he would've gone away for good. You can do that sort of thing. I can't. I really admire you but I'm not like you.' Her eyes glazed over for a second and then she blinked. 'I'm so sorry to barge in like this.'

'You're not barging in. It's fine. You can come round here any time.'

'Us Yorkshire women have got to stay together, eh?'

I thought she might cry so for once I went along with her. 'Here's a good Yorkshire way of solving your problem.'

'What's that?'

'I'll put the kettle on.'

Lily laughed and rubbed her eyes. 'Thanks. I could murder a cuppa. Seriously though, if you're expecting Teiji to come round later, after work—'

Is it Lucy's imagination or did Lily really ask about Teiji so often that night?

I made tea and carried it through. Lily couldn't drink hers without at least two heaped teaspoons of sugar and had to dash out to the convenience store to buy some. I never buy sugar. I eat sweet food once or twice a year, and that is plenty.

I blew gently on the hot surface of the tea between sips. Lily seemed calmer about Andy and accepted that she was safe in Tokyo.

'As safe as anyone ever is, anywhere.' She gulped her tea like a child drinking milk.

'Absolutely. So there is no point in worrying.'

'Yes. Lucy?'

'What?'

'I know it's stupid of me but I don't want to sleep in my own flat tonight. I know he won't come, it's just that I'm all nervous now and I'll never be able to sleep. Would it be OK if I stopped here?'

I didn't mind at all. I had extra bedding. My

flat had attained a rare cosiness that evening, with the cushions, the tea, and shared confidences. I knew already that if Lily left I would be suddenly lonely and my flat would be bare again. I hadn't seen Teiji for seven days. Busy at the restaurant. The previous couple of nights had been long and solitary. Stupid, ugly Lucy had slept fitfully in her cold bed. Every time she woke during the night the feeling that she had somehow made Teiji stop loving her came afresh and kicked her hard in the stomach.

We pulled the futons out of the cupboard and laid them side by side. We turned our backs on one another and slept. I am sure that without disturbances we would both have slept soundly until the morning, but that was not the case. In the middle of the night there was a sharp jolt. The walls shook and one of the teacups slipped from the table and rolled across the floor. I sat up, rubbed my eyes, and saw that Lily was already sitting under my desk. The street lamp outside shone through the window and bathed her in a yellow light. She hugged her knees tightly against her chest. Her eyes were shut, screwed up like raisins.

'Lily. Are you all right?'

'I'm scared.'

'It's not such a bad one.' I paused. 'I think it's stopped.'

The floor shuddered again.

'What's that noise?'

I hadn't been conscious of it until she mentioned it. Then I realized the sound had been there all along, since before I woke up, somewhere in my sleep.

'The earthquake bird.'

'The what?'

As I listened for it the noise faded and I knew the room had stopped moving.

'I don't know what it is. It's always there in a quake. I thought it was a piece of old metal being knocked against something. It sounds too far away to be anything moving in the petrol station, though. Teiji thinks it's a bird, some old night bird being knocked off its perch by the jolt.'

'Sounded like a boot kicking an old tin can somewhere in the distance.'

'Who'd be kicking an old can outside my flat every time there happens to be an earthquake?'

'Good point.'

'The thing is, every time I listen more closely to work it out, I get confused. It's hard to judge in the middle of the night. And as soon as I'm awake enough to concentrate, it's stopped. If you and Teiji hadn't heard it too, I'd think I was dreaming.'

What I didn't tell Lily about the earthquake bird was that I'd noticed something else. It didn't start at the same time as the rocking. It started just before. Was that a dream? If so, it was always the same. How could the bird, or tin can, or boot, know an earthquake was about to happen? I pondered on this many times. I could have been wrong of course. Nothing is certain in the middle of the night. But if I was right, was it a warning or a symptom? If it was a warning, of what use was it just a few seconds before the event, with no time to run or hide?

Tonight my bed may be in this police station. What noises will I hear? Sirens, perhaps, police gossip. Drunkards being locked up. I had imagined that the inside of a police station would be dark. It isn't but I wish it were. This room is painfully bright. My eyes are tired and I would like to sleep a little.

In the morning I made tea and put it on the floor beside Lily's head.

'Thank you. Ooh, I slept like a log. I don't think I woke up once after my head hit the pillow.'

'Except for the earthquake.'

'Earthquake? Was there a tremor last night? I must have slept through it.'

'No, you were awake. We both were.'

'Must have dropped straight off again, then. Don't remember a thing.'

It's easy to forget things that happen in the night when you're half asleep. I thought it odd though that she had no recollection of getting out of bed and hiding under the table, no memory of our conversation about the earthquake bird.

We walked to the station together. She was bright and chirpy and didn't mention the previous night, or Andy. From the station I caught the train to work and she went home to get changed before heading for the bar.

At work, I found a letter on my desk. The stamps on the envelope were British but I didn't recognize the round, neat handwriting. The only person in Britain who knew my work address was Lizzie. We never wrote letters and I had no idea what she was doing now but we sent each other Christmas cards every two or three years with just a signature. Lizzie's handwriting was long and spidery, though. For a stupid moment I thought the letter could have come from Lily's boyfriend, but he couldn't know who I was, or where I worked.

I tore open the envelope and pulled out the letter. I stared at the signature for several seconds before I was able to read the whole page. It was from Jonathan, the second youngest of my remaining brothers. I hadn't heard from any of them since before I left home. I assumed the cause of this letter was either a joke or a death.

Dear Lucy

It has been a very long time since any of us received news from you. We are all fine and we hope you are too. Your old schoolfriend, Lizzie, gave me this address and I trust my letter will reach you. I bumped into her at Waterloo Station not long ago. She's doing very well for herself at the BBC, as some high-flying executive, but perhaps you already know that. I remember you two used to be very close.

Mum doesn't get about much these days. Her arthritis is bad though she is as sharp in mind as ever. My wife, Felicity, pops in every Tuesday and Sunday to see how she is and give her a

casserole or an apple crumble. You'll be surprised
to learn that Mum is something of a poet these
days and has had a few of her creative dabblings
appear in print in the local Recorder. We're all
very proud of her as you can imagine.

I have made a few changes in my own life.
I suppose you won't think of them as changes
because you don't know what I was doing
before. Let me fill you in. I was enjoying a career
in the police force for several years and looking
forward to my promotion when the whole course
of my life shifted on its axis. You see, I found the
Lord. It happened quite suddenly and
unexpectedly while I was pruning a rose bush
and saw a beautiful blackbird hopping along the
wall beside me. I understood for the first time
in my life that such a perfect creature must have
been created by someone and was not just a freak
of nature or product of so-called evolution.
Moreover, we seemed to know each other, as if
we'd been together once in some other world.
I left the police force after that and am now with
the Church, training to be a minister. It was the
right decision. I met Felicity in the choir stalls
and we married last year. She's the head
chorister and has a lovely voice. We are very

happy together and hoping to hear the patter of little feet in the not-too-distant future.

It is on my conscience, Lucy, that I have you – a sister created for me by Him – and yet I don't even know you. It would be nice to hear from you one day and learn of all your adventures out there in the mysterious Orient.

Let me close this letter with a poem written by Mum. She didn't say why she wrote it but I feel sure that it's about you and how she wishes you would walk back into our lives. I think you'll find it very touching.

Yours in Him,

Jonathan

The poem was on a separate sheet of paper, folded. I opened it and then folded it again, without reading the poem. I sat at my desk for twenty minutes or so, drumming my fingers, unable to do anything else. Finally, I slid the paper out of the envelope, prised it slowly open, and began to read.

Evenings With No Comfort
by Miriam Fly

Evenings bring me no comfort now
Just tea from my favourite cup

As I sit in my old, old chair
And my arthritis plays me up
There is no sound of children playing
Or laughter in the rooms
I'm living in a haunted house
With a garden full of tombs

The door is always open though
And I wish that you'd come through it
To bring a little welcome light
And not to say I blew it

Though I know I did

I laughed aloud at Miriam's doggerel, decided the poem was more likely to have been written about wanting Felicity to arrive in the doorway with one of her casseroles than about Lucy coming home.

My feelings toward Jonathan were a little more complicated. I wasn't impressed that his attempt to befriend me was transparently part of a larger scheme to befriend God, at least for long enough to get a job out of Him. Still, it's always exciting to receive an airmail letter, in its fat, stamp-covered envelope. It's impossible to begrudge the writer at least a little gratitude. But I put the letter in a drawer and resolved to do nothing about it at present. I would take it out again in a few months and decide whether or not to send a Christmas card. I wondered if Jonathan had given my address to Miriam. I hoped not. I wished her no ill and hoped that the arthritis wasn't too painful, but I had no intention of going to see her. And I didn't want any more poems.

I returned to my work. I'd been given a difficult translation to do and a time limit of three weeks. It was a set of lengthy manuals on the production of a new type of electric wheelchair and I could not make head or tail of the diagrams. I don't normally mind long and boring translations but this one was causing me great annoyance. It had been written badly in Japanese and I had to spend a day studying the engineering of wheelchairs in order to grasp the instructions. I even constructed a model wheelchair using paper cups, an old birthday card and a couple of toothpicks. The air-conditioning blew it repeatedly to the floor until I smashed it up and threw it away. Every day for three weeks I worked from early morning until it was time to catch the last train home.

*

I didn't see Lily or Teiji during those weeks. I wanted to see Teiji but when I wasn't working, I was sleeping. There was no time. He was on my mind, though, and as I worked at the translation I counted down the days until I would be with him again. The only person I spoke to was Natsuko. She was busy too but we had our lunches together, shared complaints about dictionaries and badly drawn diagrams.

One lunchtime, in the middle of all this, Natsuko suggested we go for a quick walk.

'I want to show you something,' she said.

That is one of my favourite sentences. I didn't mind that the thing might be nothing, or something bad. Just those words were enough to give me that exquisite feeling that reminds me of lights going down in an auditorium, ready for the thrill to begin.

I followed Natsuko out to the street, almost skipping as I went. The streets were packed. Shibuya is teeming with teenagers every hour of the day, every day of the week. It is enough to make a thirty-four-year-old feel ancient. Why were these kids never in school? We pushed through the crowds of wedged heels and pink mobile phones until we emerged in a little side street. Here there were just two small shops. One sold potted plants, another vintage clothing. Apart from these it was a calm, quiet, residential area. Apartment buildings next to old garages next to small houses.

'You'll love this.' Natsuko was confident in everything she said. And her confidence is always justified. I have never known her to be wrong, though I can see her deliberating now on my role in Lily's death. 'I discovered it last week. I came round here looking for a hairdresser's someone told me about but I couldn't find it. I'm glad I got lost, though. Look.'

She had climbed onto an overturned bucket on the street and was peering over the stone wall of a private garden. Her frizzy ponytail stuck out behind her. She stared for a minute or two, jumped down.

'You have a look.'

From the ground I could see that the small garden contained a couple of ragged pine trees. I could make out flowers of pink and white through a gap in the wall. A ginger cat came and rubbed its back against my legs, looked up at me, mewed. I stroked it until it was bored and went to Natsuko for affection. I stepped onto the bucket.

In the centre of the garden was a camellia tree.

It had shiny green leaves, pale pink clusters of petals that looked as though blood was pumped into them through tiny capillaries. Its dark branches were so beautifully curved, so perfectly distanced from one another that it looked like a tree from a story book, a tree that would hold strange, magical properties if you rubbed a branch or nibbled a leaf.

'I've never seen a camellia tree so beautiful.' Natsuko had poked one eye and her nose through the gap in the wall. 'I just want to stand here and look at it all day.'

Lucy hasn't always had a happy relationship with trees but it isn't fair to condemn all for the crimes of one.

'It's lovely.' I looked for another minute or so. The image of the tree will always be inside my head, not because it was beautiful – though it was – but because it made Natsuko so incredibly happy and because she took me to see it.

'Thank you for bringing me.'

'My pleasure. If I ever have my own house, I want a tree like that in the garden. I suppose I'd have to buy this house. There can't be another tree just like this one. I'd like to look for one, though.

But if I had this tree I'd be happy for ever. If I had this tree, I wouldn't want anything else.'

Natsuko was a natural smiler, as Lucy has mentioned, but on that short break from our cramped office her smile used up her whole face, her mouth, eyes, cheekbones, nose and chin. Even her bouncy fringe had extra spring in it. I think it was infectious because, as we returned to the office, I felt a little lighter on my feet.

I finished the wheelchair translation on the day of the deadline. I went home and called Teiji, hoping to see him soon. He couldn't come to the phone. He was busy and would be working in the restaurant every night for the next few weeks. I was bitterly disappointed. I wondered if he was really so busy or if he was still brooding about Lucy opening his boxes, looking at his photographs. Or Sachi. Had I somehow brought her back by yanking her from her place in the middle of the box and out into the open air? Was he with Sachi now, or thinking about her?

But perhaps I was being unfair. I had been genuinely busy at work for the same period of time. There was no reason why Teiji shouldn't also have to work hard. I sat in my flat feeling bored and lonely, trying not to think of Jonathan and Felicity, or Miriam in her old, old chair with her apple crumble. I wondered whether or not to call Lily.

And then the phone rang. It was Lily. She was calling to tell me that she would be leaving Japan at the end of the month.

'Why?'

'I don't belong here. I should go home and face up to my life. I need to get back to nursing. I'm so bad at being a barmaid. Everything just goes wrong.'

'But what about Andy?'

'I might not bump into him.'

'Of course you will. What are you talking about? You don't want to walk right back into the problems you left, do you?'

'Maybe I've been hard on him.' She spoke in a soft voice, slightly soppy. 'I miss him a bit. I was all right when I wasn't thinking about him but now I am, he's got right under my skin again. I've suddenly started to get really homesick and I want to go back. Tokyo will never be my home.'

'Whatever you want.' I slammed the phone down and wondered why I was so upset. It had nothing to do with me. I should have been glad to be rid of her.

The truth was, I had grown used to having her around. She made me feel competent, at home in Tokyo, clever. And something else. When I was alone at night and closed my eyes, I always remembered the moment when I tumbled on the mountainside, the sharp pain in my ankle. That memory would then lead to deeper thoughts, of all the people I'd lost, the disasters I'd caused. And then the touch of fingers as Lily made me better. Her warm nurse's hands soothed me to sleep and were there should I fall again. I didn't want her to go.

But I was not motivated by pure selfishness. I became depressed on Lily's behalf at the thought of her return to Hull and Andy, for Lucy cannot hear of another person's plan without living through it in her head. However I conjured it in my brain, Andy and Lily were bound for a sticky end. Lily had tasted escape and to return to captivity would never work. No, this was a bad plan and it became Lucy's purpose to keep Lily in Japan, at least for a little longer.

I had an idea. An idea of a place. Could there be a better place in Japan for Lucy and Lily to visit than the one I had just thought of? This rugged island in the north had provided exile for criminals and the politically undesirable for centuries. It was perfect for these two modern-day exiles. I called her back.

'Come to Sado Island with me.'

'Where?'

'It's an island in the Japan Sea. I've always wanted to go there and now I'm going. Please come with me. It's a beautiful place – I've read about it – with lots of temples and clear blue sea. Mrs Katoh, my friend who played the viola, was from there and I've wanted to visit ever since. We could spend time in Niigata too, in the mountains, if you wanted to. You can't leave Japan until you've been somewhere outside Tokyo, and that doesn't include the piddly hill we climbed in Yamanashi.'

'Well, when?'

'A month from now. For a long weekend.'

'Is it far?'

'Yes, quite far. That's why we're going to go there. It's far from Tokyo.'

'It's very tempting. Won't you want to go with Teiji, though?'

'I don't know.' I really didn't know. 'I can't imagine him outside Tokyo, but he might want to. Never mind that, what about you?'

'I think I'd like to go. Yes, I would.'

'That's settled, then. No thoughts of leaving Japan for at least another month.'

I replaced the receiver, pleased with myself.

Nine

'Teiji, there's something I'd like to do.' I pressed play on his CD player to set off the music he liked to listen to, electronic jazz. 'I want to go to a party with you.'

I didn't like parties especially, though I enjoyed loud music and alcohol. In my student days I went to parties only to find men who would be drunk enough to sleep with me. I hated all the small-talk in the kitchen and the queue for the bathroom. I was bored by the tears and tantrums of the rejected, the needless waste of energy. Lucy went to parties with a clear purpose. It was simple enough. You won or you lost, and if you lost you tried again next time. My feelings hadn't changed and I'd never felt inclined to go to parties in Tokyo particularly, but I thought Teiji might want to. He'd spent nights and nights at parties with Sachi.

Teiji was at the kitchen sink, washing up his

only cup. It was pale green and chipped. He rinsed it carefully and turned to look at me, holding it in both hands as if it were something precious.

'Or a club?' I was making myself nervous.

'If you want to. We could go to a club tonight. What kind of place were you thinking of?'

'I don't know.'

He laughed. 'You should think of where you're going before you suggest going there.'

'I thought— There are places you used to go to.'

He sighed, picked up a tea towel and began to dry the cup. He didn't speak for a moment, then walked over to where I knelt by the CD player.

'With Sachi. I know. I don't want to go to those places any more. She's not here and it would feel strange. Anyway, I don't want to. If you'd like to go out then I've got an idea. I know a new jazz club not too far from here. One of our customers is always going. He says it's small and cosy, a bit unusual.'

'You never mentioned it before.'

'I only heard about it a couple of days ago. I didn't know you'd be interested.'

'I am. It sounds good.'

It was the first time Teiji and I had really planned

to go somewhere together and it felt like a date. I don't wear make-up and I don't have nice clothes, but I glanced in the mirror before we left, smoothed down my hair and gave my reflection a saucy wink.

It didn't matter how we looked. The place was so dark that once we were seated we could barely make out the other tables. The walls disappeared into blue-black shadows and, though the room was small, it was hard to see where it ended. The piano and sax played in a dim, dusty light. Though there couldn't have been more than a few metres between us, the light made them seem far away. Their music was melancholic and caressing. It warmed me like a hot toddy, gave me the kind of feeling that makes my face settle into a smile before I even know I'm happy.

Teiji's skin shimmered in the light of our tiny candle, like the surface of ice melting, and I remembered our first meeting when he looked like water. The very thought turned me on with a sharp thrill. Teiji, my ice statue-man. I sipped my gin and savoured the taste, the touch of the glass stalk between my fingers. My other hand went under the table, smoothed along Teiji's trousers. I felt him go hard.

I stroked gently and took another sip of gin. Teiji tilted his head toward me with a crooked smile, brushed his lips across my face and kissed my cheek. He slid his fingertips into my jeans, into me, so that I sucked my tongue, and then we kissed, slipped off our cushioned chairs to the dark floor where Teiji lay on his back, raised his arms to welcome me, and I fucked him. The last of my gin spilled on his face and I licked it off with the plaintive music of the saxophone in my ears. In our dark corner no one noticed us, or cared to stop us. It almost seems that it was intended to be this way, that it was the whole point of the club's darkness, the waiters' invisible service. I admit, I half hoped we would be caught. I thought Sachi had gone, finally. I wanted the world to know that Teiji was mine.

I still can't find Teiji's voice clearly in my head and so I have been approximating his language, but there are words that are never forgotten because they repeat themselves so vividly, so many times, after their utterance. The next morning Teiji said something with such clarity I can't erase it from my memory. He was lying beside me when I awoke, watching me. The camera was not in sight.

'You are a bit strange,' he said.

Did he say it in English or Japanese? If it was English the word 'strange' may not be so bad. In an individualistic society it could be taken as a compliment. But if he spoke to me in Japanese he probably said I was *hen*, which is not so nice. English or Japanese. The more I think the less I remember. And I doubted the notion that it is possible to be only *a bit* strange. Surely one is strange or one is not. The look on his face had worried me. He looked nervous, perhaps even afraid. I had no answer, in either language.

Lucy had been told she was strange since she was about five years old. Being strange was normal for Lucy so she had no understanding of what strangeness was, or why she had it. But that morning she knew that she was going to lose Teiji. From his expression she knew that he didn't feel as close to her as she had believed. She didn't try to argue or disprove his opinion. Nor did she ask him what he meant. It could have been argued that Teiji was himself more than a little unconventional – wandering around in the night taking pictures of nothing and showing them to nobody, for instance – and he had no business calling the kettle black. But that didn't occur to Lucy at the time because

Teiji was simply Teiji. It was not a question of normality or strangeness. She could have laughed to see if he laughed too and it was all a joke. But it didn't feel like a joke. She closed her eyes and pretended to be asleep.

Much later she went home and didn't go to his flat the next night because she was afraid that he wouldn't be there, or that he would call from his balcony and tell her to go away because she was being too strange down there.

I made my plans for Sado Island and decided that I would see Teiji again when I returned, try to repair the damage I'd caused. There was a reason for Teiji's observation, you see. His remark, 'You are a bit strange,' came not from nowhere. He didn't awaken in the early hours and suddenly realize that the woman beside him was disconcertingly original. Lucy prompted the remark herself, with a story she had told him the night before, when we returned from the jazz club feeling sexy but also rather seedy. It was this story, I believe, that caused Teiji to stay awake all night and stare at me while I, having thrown off my burden, slept like a baby. In the morning, when I awoke, he stared at me and said, 'You are a bit strange,' and I didn't understand what he meant.

What I had chosen to share with him was my very first sexual encounter, Lucy's first crunch into the apple. I told him because, when he lay beside me in bed, I thought of Sachi again and my theft of her secrets. I thought I could return some of the confidence I stole that evening with a disclosure of my own. I also believed that he would fall asleep, as he had the previous time I told him my stories, and not hear a word.

Lucy was even less attractive as a teenager than she is now, and with a more hostile audience to play to, the boys didn't follow her and she didn't want them to. She was interested only in her cello and her secret languages. She came to accept that having a boyfriend was a thing some girls did, and some did not. In the same way, Lucy knew that wearing make-up and fashionable clothes was not her destiny.

One Sunday afternoon, when Lizzie was sick in bed with hypochondria, Lucy found herself at the door of another classmate. The girl's name was Caroline and Lucy had, she believes now, reason to knock on the door about a geography project.

The geography teacher was always setting pointless tasks, such as calculating the amount of wheat needed to make enough bread to feed all of East Yorkshire. Lucy considered hers a poor education, parochial and irrelevant. They never taught her the map of the world, the names of the countries and what you would find if you visited. The only reason she knew her atlas so well, able to name the capital city of every country when she was thirteen, was that she put in hours of study at night. Other pupils in her class didn't know the Isle of Wight from Australia yet gained high grades because they could correctly distinguish between four kinds of pig. Lucy learned the main cities, the small towns, the languages, the music of country after country, but refused to pay more than minimal attention to local agricultural issues as a matter of principle. She was satisfied with her self-education though a little perturbed to discover, many years later, that the atlas under her bed was an old one. Dreamy places such as Ceylon, Formosa, Persia and Siam now went under different, less exotic names.

She entered the house, following shy Caroline through the bacon-smelling hall to the back room. Caroline's father walked in from the garden, greeted them with a hearty hello. He was foreign.

In the small village of Lucy's childhood, this was a most distinguishing feature. There were few foreigners around, and he was so casual about it. She had heard in the Co-op that he was Russian but when he came to Britain he took on an English name, Brian Church. Caroline always denied that he was anything but British, despite the giveaway of his accent. Lucy had read about Russia and believed that Brian Church's real name was Boris Chekhov. She had sometimes heard him speaking in the local shops, a gravelly voice, a voice of spies and vodka. She would listen from the other side of the aisle in the Co-op as he talked with another shopper about the price of bread. She longed to hear him speak of Russia but he never did. So it was with excitement that she sat in his back room with her geography project under her arm, and returned his hello.

He left the room immediately and Lucy's eyes scoured the room for Russian dolls, ballet shoes, bearskins, anything.

There is a gap in the story where Lucy cannot remember exactly what happened, but presumes she worked on the project with Caroline. They must have discussed wheat or corn, found something to write. Perhaps they drew a plan of a farm. But she knows what happened after that.

She was upstairs on the landing, outside the bathroom. She had tried the door but found it locked. The toilet flushed and Caroline's father came out, drying his hands on the sides of his trousers. He smiled through butter-yellow teeth and apologized. She took that moment to stare at him with her piercing eyes, into his pupils that were Russian and had seen another life and country.

She wanted to see his life, to read it like a book.

He looked back at her, puzzled. His heavy brow was furrowed and his lips tight. Beads of sweat began to gather just above his eyebrows. He followed her into the bathroom and with a few grunts, rid her of the virginity she had so long been saddled with. When Lucy left the house twenty minutes later, she was sore and had the shape of a tap embedded in her thigh, like a tattoo.

For the next couple of weeks I thought I had become half-Russian. I called myself Olga, secretly, and named the baby I believed was growing inside me Natasha. Those were fraught and exciting days. But Caroline didn't come to school one morning and I learned that her father had set off to sea the previous afternoon in his canoe. He hadn't bothered to paddle back again and his body had washed up on the shore in the evening. I went from being half-Russian to being half-dead. And there was no baby inside. There was nothing at all. When the incident was reported in the local newspapers, Lucy discovered that Brian Church had not come from Russia, but from the Netherlands.

Teiji had one arm around my head as I told my story. He brushed his nose against my cheek so that the hairs on my skin tingled. When I reached the part about Brian Church's suicide, he pulled away a little. I hardly noticed except that my face went cold. I wondered if perhaps I had said too much, but then I was asleep.

There was cool air between us the next day. He tried not to show I had shocked him, but I knew. He took a picture of me when we walked to the station in the afternoon, but it was not the same. The click of the shutter wasn't a natural part of his movement, his usual unconscious action. He peered through the viewfinder, moved around preoccupied, frowned irritably and then, resigned, took the picture.

'Teiji,' I said. But I had no more words to follow. I didn't know what I could say to him because I had no idea what he was thinking. It might have been that I was so young, that Brian Church was so old, that I drove a man to suicide, that I fucked a schoolfriend's father, that Teiji couldn't bear the fact that I'd ever slept with another man. He may have thought that, like Sachi, Brian Church belonged to the past and it was wrong to bring him back. Now there'd be no getting rid of him.

Teiji fixed his brown, translucent eyes on my face, perhaps hoping for a reversal of the previous night, something to put my story back where I'd found it. But that was beyond Lucy's control.

Ten

Sado Island is situated in the unlucky north-east
and equally unlucky north-west, depending on
where you are and who you are. In olden times,
when Kyoto was the capital, anything north-east
of the city could bring it bad luck, so that included
Sado Island. I learned this fact from Mrs Katoh
who, leaving her husband and son behind on the
island, had come to Tokyo in search of some good
luck. The island, being located so unluckily, is for-
tified against the bad spirits by numerous temples.
I thought about this often. Perhaps Mrs Katoh's
relentless giggle was also fortification against
badness. Or perhaps she started laughing when she
first arrived in Tokyo, or when she found Mrs
Yamamoto and the house with wisteria over the
door and music inside. But for me it was different.
If you're starting from Tokyo, Sado is in the north-
west and this direction was more unlucky for Lucy.

She had read *Kinkakuji*, and identified with the tragic monk who was told by a fortune-teller not to travel to the north-west because it would bring bad luck, so he did. I was not deterred from going north-westerly; if anything the bad luck pulled me in that direction. Like the ugly, stammering Mizoguchi, I could not but think of myself as connected in some way to a place that was so prone to malevolence.

Lily was waiting for me on the platform at Tokyo station. We were taking the shinkansen to Niigata and there we would board a ferry to the island. I had told Teiji of our plans but didn't expect him to come. As far as I knew, Teiji had not been outside Tokyo since he'd arrived, aged fourteen, to meet Uncle Soutaro for the first time. Why would he want to? With his camera and his long, solitary nights on the streets, he had come to understand Tokyo as a limitless form, a voice that called him then ran away and hid. For Teiji, each street, or bridge, or river was another connection in the spiral he was bidden to follow, outward and outward without ever finding the end. Why would he want to disprove this truth so comically by getting on a train and travelling out to the city's physical edge and beyond, seeing the clear line where Tokyo stops and the countryside begins? And of course, I thought he wouldn't want to be with me. I was too strange.

Some part of Lucy's thesis was wrong, for two minutes after finding Lily and leading her to the correct part of the platform, I spotted Teiji. He had just come through the ticket barriers and was waving at me. I jumped up in the air with joy. Lily squeezed my arm.

When he reached me, I hugged him. Hugging Teiji was not like a normal embrace because he didn't respond in the usual way. He didn't hug back but neither did he stand coldly as if being embraced by an old aunt. It was something in-between that I couldn't fathom. I put my arms around him, squeezed only slightly – just enough to feel the unique fingerprint of his warmth and muscles – and pulled back so as not to risk making him uncomfortable.

'I never thought you'd come,' I said.

'I miss the sea.' He inhaled deeply as if he could already smell it. 'I used to love the ocean but I never go there any more. And I didn't want you to go without me.'

I smiled at that and I think his words repeated themselves all the way to Sado.

The journey led us away from the industrial pulse of Japan and toward the green paddy fields and hills of the countryside. I forced Lily to study Japanese by pointing out features we passed and getting her to repeat the Japanese names. At first she didn't want to.

'It's too hard. Look at me. I haven't even got O-level French.'

'Never mind, this is Japanese and you're not taking your O-levels today. Look over there. See? That's a *mori*.'

'Where, what?'

'Guess,' said Teiji. He was sitting on the other side of the aisle. He turned in his seat to join in the lesson, rested one foot over the other. His trousers were baggy, looked as though there were no legs inside them, just crumpled cotton.

Lily blushed. She didn't mind being bad at Japanese with me, but in front of a Japanese person she was acutely self-conscious. Lucy has this syndrome in reverse. I've never minded making mistakes when I'm speaking to a native Japanese speaker, but if a non-Japanese person is listening, I like to be word-perfect.

'That – the mountain?' She pointed her finger

feebly at one of the many high peaks that spread toward the skyline.

'That's a *yama*.' Teiji was a gentle teacher. He corrected so well that you learned both words – the wrong one and the right one – and never forgot them.

'*Yama*. The trees, then. *Mori* means tree?'

'Almost. That's very close. Have another guess.' I was enjoying the lesson. It was like watching a child learn to identify simple objects for the first time.

'The leaves on the trees?'

'Nope. Leaves are *ha*.'

'That's easy to remember. Ha ha, it's a leaf.' She was pleased with the notion and smiled at her cleverness.

'But you could forget and say, ha ha it's a branch.' Teiji grinned.

'Why would you say either?' I didn't think this was helping Lily. 'You might as well say ha ha it's a pavement or ha ha it's a bus stop.'

'Don't confuse me. Branch. Is *mori* a branch?'

'Branch is *eda*.'

'*Yama*, *eda*, *ha*. OK, I've got those. I give up. What does *mori* mean?'

'Not telling. You have to work it out for yourself.'

Thick forests spread over the mountains, dark green and fuzzy. There was nothing else to see. I wondered if Lily had a sight problem.

'I'll give you a hint.' Teiji fumbled in his pockets, then in his rucksack.

'What are you looking for?'

'Have you got a pen or pencil and paper?'

'I haven't.' Lily shrugged. 'I never carry anything except my purse and my hairspray. And my undies of course, when I'm going away. And a toothbrush and—'

'Here.' I handed Teiji a chewed pencil and a shopping receipt.

On the back of the receipt Teiji wrote the kanji for *mori*, twelve simple but deft strokes, neatly drawn.

'This is how we write *mori*. What does it look like to you?'

'A Japanese letter.'

'Look at the shape.'

Lily peered at the character, the three radicals forming a triangle. 'Trees. Three little trees.'

Teiji put his finger over two of the trees and left the top one showing. 'This one alone is a tree. So what do three together mean?'

'Lots of trees. A forest?'

'You're a good student,' Teiji said, and handed me the pencil. I think we were both relieved she had got it right.

I dozed a little after that, listened to Lily repeating her new words as the things went by.

'*Yama, hashi, ki, eda, eki, ha, mori.*'

Mountain, bridge, tree, branch, station, leaf, forest.

The hills gave way to steep mountains and finally we were in Niigata. We headed straight for the port and boarded the ferry. True holiday spirit had caught us and we ran to find the best place on deck to watch mainland Japan disappear. We were leaving Honshu and heading in the direction of bad fortune to the storm-beaten land of exiles. I was deliriously happy.

The journey took over an hour and the sea was

calm. It was late afternoon when we arrived on Sado. The ferry came to a stop in the fishing town of Ryotsu and we climbed off. Lily stared at the dark mountains rising behind the town. She looked left then right, then left again trying to take their harsh beauty into her big, blank eyes. Teiji turned back to face the sea, the rugged bay we had just entered. He laughed, walking dizzily backward. A gust of wind caught him and he spun around with his arms out. He staggered suddenly and looked as if he were about to fall, but before his knees could hit the ground he leapt up again. He reminded me of the Scarecrow in *The Wizard of Oz*. I laughed at him.

In Ryotsu we walked down little back streets, breathing fishy air. We ran round corners, peeked through the windows of small wooden houses. Teiji picked up a discarded piece of fishing net and chased me through the sleepy streets. People looked at us and smiled. No one seemed to mind his small act of theft. Lily shouted behind, 'Don't throw it over her. She'll stink of fish. Don't hurt her!'

I ran and hid between two houses. When Teiji came toward me I knew he'd lost my trail but I wasn't sure what to do. He still had the net.

I charged out behind him and tried to wrestle it from his arms. He turned suddenly and with a wide smile on his face, the widest I ever saw, he pulled the net over both our heads and pushed me gently back into my hiding place. I pushed back but he was too strong for me.

'I've caught you now,' he said. 'You'll never escape.' And he tried to kiss me but something fell off the net above his head, brushed down his cheek and touched his shoulder. He must have thought it was some kind of animal or insect because he jumped with a cry of horror and slapped his neck several times. It fell to the ground. It was a tiny strand of rope from the net. I laughed so hard I fell over and pulled Teiji down with me. Lily ran up, out of breath, to find us in a heap on the ground, struggling through laughter to get free of the net. She blushed and stepped back.

'Sorry.'

'It's OK. We're not doing anything,' I said.

'We're just laughing.' Tears ran down Teiji's cheeks. I wiped them off and rubbed them into my hands to keep them there.

Lily helped us up and we returned the net. We had planned to rent a car to tour the island and we followed signs to a place where we could get a cheap one. When we arrived, we all found ourselves looking at the shop next door, at its display of rental mopeds and bicycles.

'That would be fun,' Lily said.

'Being in a car is a bit claustrophobic.' Teiji could not take his eyes off the mopeds. 'I don't mind when there's no alternative, but . . .'

I wanted the pleasure of riding through the plains of the island, along the coastal road, by myself, not in a car sharing my air with two people. Lucy and the bike in mountain and sea air. Her two friends riding with her, but also on their own.

So we rented mopeds and set off away from Ryotsu to the road leading to the Sotokaifu coast. From there we rode by the sea until we reached Nyuukawa. We continued a little further toward the northern cape and stopped at our destination.

I had made a reservation with a minshuku, a simple, traditional inn. Our room overlooked the Japan Sea, and as soon as we'd left our bags and shoes we went down to the rocks and sand. We said we would have a look at the sea and when we saw it we said we'd have a paddle in the water. The evening was dark but the edge of the sea was lit by a few street lamps on the shore. We paddled in the small waves at the sea's edge. The cold water splashed around our tired feet. The sand between the rocks was soft and disappeared under our footsteps, like another kind of water.

Lily ran as she paddled and I followed, laughing. I don't remember where Teiji was. I rolled up the legs of my jeans, but the water splashed up to my thighs and soaked me. I laughed harder. Lily shouted something at me but I didn't catch it. She twisted around, still running, to repeat it, but as she did so, tripped over her own leg and fell backward into the water. I could not contain myself. I choked with laughter till I thought my chest would explode. I didn't dare look at Lily in case she was hurt for I knew that even if she was, I would not be able to stop laughing. I started to drag myself to the sand but as I turned my back on the water there was a loud splash behind me and I was being pulled into the sea. Lily had grabbed my shoulders, forcing me to take two steps back. Then she settled her arms around my waist and threw me down. I coughed and spat salty water back into the sea, looked up to find Lily. She was grinning.

'That'll learn you,' she shrieked, and ran off inviting me to chase her. Her red tuft of hair that never flinched in the wind had been flattened by the sea. Her face looked quite different, less silly, older. She kicked up water as she ran so I couldn't get closer to her. I didn't try. I just flipped over and turned cartwheel after cartwheel along the wet sand. Gentle waves licked my hands, my feet, and then my hands again. I was delighted that I could still keep my legs up straight after a retirement of about twenty-five years.

I don't remember stopping but I know that a little later Lily and I were walking along the beach side by side. Our voices were quick and breathy. My face and hands tingled with a cold that stung so sharply it was almost warmth.

Lily put out her arm and motioned for me to stop. I looked to where she silently pointed. On the beach a few feet away from us was a small bundle of clothes. Of course, I recognized Teiji's baggy cotton trousers and white T-shirt immediately. On top of them, held down by a smooth grey stone, were his shorts.

I looked back at the sea. Small waves shivered under the weak moonlight, as far as I could see in each direction. Then I saw Teiji, a white featureless stick moving slowly through the water. He ducked between the waves and turned every now and then from his front to his back. He was relishing the touch of water on his bare skin.

The sight was so beautiful that I wanted to stand on the shore and watch Teiji for as long as he was there, but Lily appeared at my shoulder with a giggle.

'He's got the right idea.' Her voice was full of thrill. She waved at Teiji though he didn't notice her, then pulled off her knickers and brandished them with a whoop. She unzipped her dress and slipped it off in one movement. When she stepped out of it she gave a self-conscious shiver and turned to the water's edge, hesitated. I understood her dilemma. It was too cold to go straight in up to her neck, but she was suddenly too aware of her nakedness to make a cautious, joint by joint entry. She waded steadily up to her knees. The whiteness of her skin was dazzling, as if lit by fluorescence. To me she didn't look like a naked woman but like a skeleton in a funfair ghost ride. Then she screwed up her face, lunged forward and screamed as her whole body went down into the icy water. I watched her disappear. The dark sea smoothed over the spot where she had been. She resurfaced a few metres away and swam, taking firm, regular strokes until she relaxed and began to twist and turn in the water. She moved further from the shore. Soon I could not tell which of the two bobbing figures was Lily and which was Teiji.

I wanted to swim too, but I had played enough games and needed to be alone with the water and night sky. I walked a little further along the edge of the sea to where the moon caught the sea in yellow patches. The cold water slapped my ankles. I left my clothes on the sand and ran in up to my shoulders. The water gripped my whole body and I kicked off, swam away from the shore beyond battered rocks that jutted out into the sea.

Every stroke and forward push was a fresh shock as the sea gnawed at my flesh like sharp-toothed, hungry fish. I kept my head up and looked at the water before me, the Sea of Japan. I guessed I was swimming north-west of the island. If I floated now, letting the water carry my frozen body, where would I finish my journey? Following my bad-luck direction, I might come to Vladivostok or Nakhodka. If I continued northerly from there, I would head to the freezing Sea of Okhotsk. I gasped with cold, tasted salt. It was exhilarating but the thought of Siberia made the water still colder. I twisted around and took a few strokes southward, toward South Korea, Shanghai, the warmer waters of the East China Sea.

My limbs were stiffening. The cold water between my legs and under my arms made every breath shorter than the last. I thought I would die if I kept swimming, and yet I also felt as if I had never been so joyously alive, so awake. The feeling wouldn't last – I knew that – but I wanted to remember it, to keep it somewhere inside to find later when I needed it back.

Of course, it didn't work. It was there and now it's gone. I need it but I can't even find the taste of the fresh air on my tongue. I can picture the water, remember that it was cold, but I'm in a stuffy room in a large building in Tokyo. It's no good remembering something if you can't live it again. It's not enough to know that I was so happy. I can't find it any more.

At the time, though, I thought it was enough. So, after carefully savouring the moment, scanning it into my memory for future use, I swam back to the shore. Lily and Teiji were side by side on the beach, picking up wet clothes to put on their dripping bodies. Convulsing with cold, they no longer cared that they were naked.

I hoped Lily would sleep well that night. I hoped that I might shift my futon closer to Teiji's and that, when Lily's breathing became heavy, I would roll over to him and, very quietly, in the warmth of snug white cotton, we would make love. I missed him.

Who unfolded the futons and laid them on the tatami? Did we each do our own or did one of us do all while the other two cleaned their teeth or undressed? I must have been sleepy for I didn't notice until we were all tucked up that Lily was lying on the middle futon. There was no way I could get to Teiji in the night without the possibility of treading on her. I couldn't blame Lily because it may not have been her fault. I might have chosen my bed first, absently forgetting my plans, or we might all have settled down at the same time. I resigned myself to a night without Teiji and accepted that I had the consolation of sleeping in the spot closest to the window. I reached for the catch and pushed it. The window slid open easily. I lay down and slept deeply to the rhythm of the waves lapping the shore.

When I awoke in the morning I was rocking gently from side to side in the warmth of yellow daylight.

Eleven

Teiji and Lily were still sleeping. I dressed, stepped over their peaceful bodies, and went outside. I would have a quiet walk before breakfast.

The sea was blue under the morning sun, but had lost none of its night-time magic. I looked out at the glinting ripples. When I turned my head back to the beach I saw, out of the corner of my eye, a canoe in the sea that had not been there before. Still looking only through the outer edge of my left eye, I was surprised but not alarmed to see the long-lost Brian Church canoeing along in the water parallel to my steps. He waved at me. It was a friendly wave as if he were pleased to see me strolling there. His paddle cut soundlessly through the water with quick movements. Yet he didn't seem to go any faster, stayed near me all the time. I didn't turn and face him directly lest he should disappear. I just walked on, for a mile or so, knowing that he was there, smiling and waving at Lucy. When I turned to retrace my steps, I permitted myself a quick glance at the water.

In the minshuku, Lily and Teiji were up and dressed. The landlady was in the room loading breakfast from large trays onto our low table. Bowls of rice, miso soup, raw eggs, salty fish. The eye of my fish looked up blankly, as if it had something to tell me but it had forgotten what it was. Lily didn't like her fish to have its head on and was particularly upset by the idea of an eye at breakfast time. She covered the eye with a piece of dry seaweed, cut off the head and handed it to me to throw down the toilet. I did so. When I came to eat my own fish I plucked the soft black eye out of its socket with the end of one chopstick, and ate it by itself. It tasted fishy.

'Full of nutrients,' I said, and picked a tiny piece of membrane from between my teeth.

'Oh my God,' Lily whispered. 'I do not believe you just did that. It's the most disgusting thing I've ever seen. You're warped.'

I might be, but I only ate the fish's eye because I knew it would horrify Lily. Normally, like anyone else, I would just pick the flesh from the bones to eat and leave the head intact.

Teiji was amused by Lily's reaction. 'The whole thing is dead.'

'But the eye—'

'You're a nurse. I didn't expect you to be squeamish. You must have dealt with gory eyes sometimes.'

'Yes, but I don't eat them.'

Teiji grinned. He wrapped seaweed around a scoop of rice and nibbled it, still smiling to himself.

Teiji and I ate heartily while Lily picked at the edges of her fish which she ate in small bites between individual grains from her rice bowl.

'Have some tea.' I poured green tea into the three small cups.

'Thanks. That's the one part of Japanese breakfast I can cope with.'

'You'll soon acquire the taste.'

'I'll have to. Since I'm planning on being here a while.'

'You're not going to leave, then? That's good news.' I was suddenly proud of my success.

'Since I'm here I might as well make the most of it, right? Now I'm learning bits of Japanese it seems more hopeful, somehow. And, more than anything, having friends makes me want to stay because now I feel as if it's OK to be here, as if I'm supposed to be here. Do you know what I mean?'

We nodded.

'But that doesn't mean I want to look at dead fishes' faces first thing in the morning. Can we get an ice cream later?'

'Why not?' Teiji drank his tea in one gulp that washed down a mouthful of rice.

'Good. What are we going to do today?'

I rattled off the list of possibilities in my guide-book and asked what sort of things they wanted to do. Lily wanted to see the sights. Teiji was less interested in museums and monuments than in the scenery, but said that he didn't mind what we did.

'I'm surrounded by water and mountains so I'm happy. I'll do whatever you want. Being here is enough.'

'There's a gold mine museum,' I said. 'It might be interesting.'

I like going underground. I like a little claustro-phobia, some darkness and a bit of panic before I come into the open again. It's important to get good value for money. I wanted to go down there into the mine so that I could imagine being buried alive, trapped for ever in a wormhole with gold-flecked wallpaper.

We planned to ride south toward Aikawa to visit the old gold mines. On the way we would stop and look at some of the cliffs and small islands. In the afternoon we might visit temples, museums, Noh theatres. We would spend the night in an inn in Mano. There would be one remaining day before returning to Tokyo.

Teiji put a new roll of film in his camera, took a quick shot of Lily and me mounting our mopeds. We rode to Senkaku-wan to see the famously beautiful stretch of cliffs. And on that journey, something happened to Lucy. An unexpected excitement caught her and she found herself riding the bike faster and faster. She knew she might lose control of the machine – when was the last time she'd been on a moped? – but couldn't tell herself to slow down. The route ahead was clear and my knuckles were white. I sped along the hard grey road with Lily and Teiji far behind. When we arrived at Senkaku-wan I stopped and nearly went over the handlebars.

I left the bike, started to walk to the cliffs but was suddenly dizzy. It may have been the journey –

I had felt a little giddy at the time – or the fish's eye I had for breakfast, or the cartwheels of the previous night. It's not like Lucy to be sick so I ignored the feeling for a while and tried to enjoy the view. But my stomach was coming up to my mouth and my knees were fading away altogether. I knew I couldn't go any further.

'Sorry,' I said to Lily and Teiji and fell to the ground. I shut my eyes and disappeared. I was vaguely aware, as I fell, of two astonished faces watching me wither and drop but I could not open my eyes again. Perhaps it was my dream or perhaps it was real when Lily put a cool hand on my forehead, pulled me onto my side and lifted my head to put something soft underneath.

'Just sleep. You'll feel better,' someone said. 'It doesn't matter. It's not your fault, you know – do you know that?' It was a female voice so I took it to be Lily's but now, when I think about it carefully, I realize it was speaking Japanese. There were no other people around. Perhaps it was not a woman's voice but Teiji's, suddenly unfamiliar.

When I reappeared, I opened my eyes slowly. The world was nothing but dots and lines that hurt my head until they slid into place. I sat up. Only a few metres away was a steep drop to the sea. The cliffs were sharp and rugged, not very friendly. I drew breath shakily. It made me feel a little better. I was alone. I looked in each direction but Lily and Teiji were not there.

I stood and walked over to my moped. The other two bikes had gone. Lily and Teiji had abandoned me. What could I do without knowing where they had gone? I realized I was carrying the object that had been my pillow. It was Teiji's T-shirt. I held it against my face. The warmth in it was all mine, not Teiji's, and it was a lonely warmth. I burst into tears. He didn't want to be with me any more, ever since he'd decided I was strange, ever since I told him of Brian Church.

'Where am I supposed to go?' I wept to the sea. 'Come back.'

I waited and waited, alternately crying and pacing the clifftop in anger. If they'd gone to get help, surely they would have returned by now. There were campsites and hostels only five minutes away.

When I was tired of waiting I headed to Kinzan, to the mining museum. The journey took me further along the coast, then uphill and along a thin winding road into the mountains. The old gold mine was nestled in the woods with a couple of tour buses parked outside the gates. I rode into the car park, got off the moped. Lily and Teiji were coming out of the museum. Teiji was wearing a new T-shirt that said 'Sado' on the front in big blue and black letters. They were laughing about something and a few moments passed before they even noticed me.

'You seem to have had a good time.' I stood in their path. They looked as if they'd been caught skiving from school.

'Lucy! We were so worried about you. Are you all right?'

'Absolutely fine. Have your T-shirt back.'

'Thank you.' Teiji took the crumpled shirt sheepishly. He knew he'd done something wrong.

Lily looked from his face to mine. 'It's a good thing we left you that note or you wouldn't have known where to find us.' She spoke brightly, so pleased that the whole day had been saved by her genius.

'What note?'

'Oh, we put a note under a stone for you. It said that we were coming here and if you didn't meet us we'd come back for you.'

'I didn't see a note.'

'It must have blown away. I'm really sorry.'

'I just came here because there was nowhere else to look for you. I could have been dying. I could have been blown off the cliff into the sea.'

I tried to make a joke of it but it came out sounding as bitter as it felt. I knew there was no note. Neither of them had been carrying a pen or paper. Teiji had borrowed them from me on the train to write the kanji for *mori* and given them back. Remember? Lucy is not stupid.

'I did check you,' Lily said. 'You were just exhausted and you'd been riding too fast. It made you woozy. It was best to let you sleep it off rather than get on the moped again and make yourself worse. You know, it's possible you've picked up some kind of virus and it's making you a bit weak.'

'Whatever you say. You're a nurse and I'm not. So I've missed the gold mine trip.'

'No, you haven't, silly. You can go in now. It's very interesting. They've got these mechanical puppets showing you what it was really like at the time. I don't mind going round again. Do you, Teiji?'

'No, not at all.' He wasn't looking at me.

'That's stupid if you two have already seen it.'

'We don't mind. Come on, let's go.' Lily turned to go back.

'No. If I go, I'll go by myself. I expect you two are anxious not to waste any more time so you'd probably better get moving. There are some very interesting temples in Mano, according to my book.'

'Don't be daft.' She took another couple of paces. 'We'll all go down the mine together. Come on.'

'And a five-storey pagoda. I'm sure you'll find it quite beautiful.'

Teiji put one hand on my elbow to lead me. 'Lucy. We'll go back in the mining museum together. We're sorry we left you.'

'No. Forget it. I don't feel like it now.' I pulled away.

I shouldn't have snapped at Teiji. Angry words were never meant for him and sulking was not a part of his language. If his mother or father had ever shouted at him he would have cycled off through the paddy fields and let the anger fall on the ground behind him. But I'm sure he had never been shouted at. In that moment I destroyed so much of what we had, at least my illusion of it, made myself sound like half of any old bickering couple. And yet. The sting had gone in deep and its poison was hurting. How could he say, *We're sorry?* Since when were Lily and Teiji announcing their apologies as a duet?

'It was just that you didn't sound keen on it when we talked about it this morning. That was why we thought you wouldn't mind if we went on without you.' Lily the conciliator. Lily the healer, the nurse.

'Yes, you're right. It doesn't matter.'

But I'd said in the morning that I wanted to go there. It was Teiji who wasn't bothered. I knew it was.

We didn't argue, didn't discuss it again. We walked in silence to our bikes and then headed to our hotel in Mano. Gradually their shame and my anger wore off and we made tentative, over-polite comments until, by late evening, we were talking almost comfortably.

In our room I made sure I was the first to the futon cupboard. I pulled out the bedding so fast that Lily and Teiji had no time to offer help. I laid one flat in the far corner.

'Lily, here you are.'

'Oh, thanks.' She threw a pillow down and went off to clean her teeth.

I put out the next one, the middle one, and

covered it with my own things. Finally, I grabbed the last one and unfolded it for Teiji.

I'd engineered the futon arrangements to my liking but I didn't sleep well that night, probably because of my extra sleep during the day. I was too hot. The muscles in my arms and legs were twitchy. I listened to Teiji and Lily breathing in and out. There was too much breathing in one room. It was oppressive. I rolled over to Teiji but couldn't relax enough to snuggle against him. I wanted Lily out of the room. Then I realized I needed Teiji to go too. I wanted to sleep by myself. I thought about dragging my bedding out of the room to sleep in the corridor, but I didn't want to wake the others and provoke interrogation. I lay for most of the night with one eye in my pillow and the other looking at the square shape of the lightshade against the dark ceiling. What I wanted was a reason for the night to be over, an interruption in the night so I could get up. What I wanted was something like an earth tremor, to shake us up, to put an end to Lily and Teiji's deep breathing sleep that was suffocating me.

I probably fell asleep at five or six in the morning. The sun had already risen when I finally dropped off.

We had planned to wander around the area of Mano, to visit temples and the museum. I was too tired to go anywhere.

'Go without me. I'll meet you later.'

They both looked nervous.

'It's not a problem. I mean, yesterday isn't a problem. It's just that I didn't sleep well last night. Until I've had a bit of sleep I don't think I can do anything.'

'You *have* got a virus. I thought so. You're very pale, you know.'

Lily put one hand on my forehead. It felt nice.

'You're a little bit hot, maybe. Well, if you're sure that's what you want to do . . .'

Teiji said, 'We'll stay here with you. It's OK.'

While I didn't relish the thought of Lily and Teiji going off together without me, I knew I wouldn't sleep unless they left.

'Please go. It's fine. I'll just have a couple more hours and then I'll join you.'

'If you're sure.' Lily looked doubtful.

Of course, they were merely putting on a slick display of politeness. They wanted me to go back to sleep and they wanted to leave the inn. They left.

*

We'd agreed to meet later at the town hall but I set off a little earlier and by chance came upon them in a different place. They were sitting on a street bench, a little back from the pavement. They were close together, not touching. Something about their silence stopped me crossing the road to greet them. I stayed on my side of the street, far enough not to be seen. Each of them was holding an ice cream. Lily licked the side of the cone where the ice cream was melting. Her tongue had the quick, delicate movement of a cat's. Teiji was crunching into the bottom part of his cone. They were not looking at each other. But Lily said something to Teiji and he reached into his pocket and pulled out a handkerchief, gave it to her. She started to wipe her fingers. She handed her half-eaten ice cream cone to him while she wiped the other hand. Teiji took the ice cream without a glance at it. He watched, casually, as she moved the handkerchief along her fingers. He licked her ice cream while he waited. This told me everything I hadn't wanted to know. They were going to sleep together. There was no stopping them.

It was the simplicity of the action that made my forehead and temples freeze. Teiji and Lily were so close that he could lick her ice cream without her offering it. They were so intimate that Lily could wipe melted ice cream all over Teiji's handkerchief and not feel the need to thank him or apologize. Lucy stared and stared and waited. She wanted to see something that would show her she was wrong, though she knew she was right.

Teiji gave the ice cream back to Lily. Lily took it. Teiji watched the cars as they passed. Lily looked up at the sky then closed her eyes, still facing upward. Teiji's handkerchief was a ball in her hand. They hardly knew each other. They should have been making polite conversation but they were silent. Lucy understood. They were so comfortable together that it was obvious. She had indeed been wrong. They had already slept together.

I walked away. I paced around the houses, faster and faster until I was lost. When did it happen? It might have been the previous morning when Lucy was walking on the beach, or later on the clifftop while she was out cold, or on some hillside, just a moped's journey away. Maybe it was during the first night when Lily slept on the middle futon and Lucy was rocking in her dreams with the sea. Or it could have happened this morning in a secret alley between houses. I went into a public toilet and tried to cry but nothing happened. When I came out I walked straight into them.

I burst out laughing.

'Lucy, how lucky. We were just on our way to meet you.'

'Yes, how lucky.' I laughed like a hyena. They laughed too, thinking I was tickled by our meeting like this, even though it was only five minutes before the appointed time and about thirty metres from the place.

I choked on my breath and coughed. I managed to steady the convulsions in my chest.

'What shall we do, then? There are so many places to visit, things to do. Let's not waste any time. Come on.'

They followed me doubtfully. 'Where are we going?'

'I don't know. There's something in every direction so let's see what we find. We can't go wrong, can we? Only if the earth turns out to be flat and we fall off the edge. Ha ha ha.'

'Lucy, what are you talking about?'

I pushed my arm through Teiji's. 'I don't know. What do you want to do? What have you already done?'

Lily answered. 'I went to *kokubunji*. A big temple. It's lovely. You two might want to see it.'

I looked at Teiji in surprise. 'You haven't seen it?'

'I went down to look at the sea, took some pictures. We bumped into each other afterwards and had an ice cream.'

'Oh.'

With my arm tightly through Teiji's, and this new piece of information, I felt better. What had I actually seen? No kiss, no touch, no sharing of secrets. No exchanges of glance or flirtatious smiles. No photograph taken of Lily by Teiji. I still trusted my initial instinct, but was ready to be proven wrong. We spent the afternoon in temples and museums. In the early evening we collected our bags and headed for the ferry. From the boat's deck I watched the jagged mountains recede. A rush of images filled my head so fast and vivid I lost sight of the sea: wooden temples, seagulls, tarmac disappearing under the moped's wheels, white futon covers and pillows, moving puppets digging for gold. I was happy to be going home.

Back at Tokyo Station Lily and I said goodbye to Teiji. He had to work late that night and early the next morning so there was no point in my going back with him. We went off in the white maze of underground passages to find our platforms. Lily was taking the Yamanote line too, but in the opposite direction. I was going clockwise, she anticlockwise. The platforms faced one another. We went up our separate staircases, said goodbye. I walked onto my platform, glanced at the overhead board to check the time of my next train. One minute to go. I looked down the length of track. The train was approaching from Kanda station. The platform was crowded and I wandered toward the rear end where there were usually fewer people. Just before my train pulled in I looked up at Lily's platform. I don't know why I looked. Perhaps if you are aware that someone you know should be standing on the next platform it's impossible not to. There was a string of people waiting. The train had not yet arrived. She should have been at the same end as me. The front of the train was nearest the exit at her station. It was also the least crowded part of her train. So why couldn't I see her?

I pushed my way back, ran along the platform against the crowds and up into the station building. I went along the passage, downstairs to Lily's platform. I ran from one end to the other, vaguely wondering what I would say to Lily if I found her calmly buying Coke from a machine. I didn't need to. Lily wasn't there.

I stumbled back up the stairs. My rucksack was bashing against my back, getting caught on the shoulders and the bags of passers-by. Briefcases hit my knees and sent me sideways. I didn't know for certain where I would find her, but there was only one direction worth trying. I found my way toward Teiji's platform. It was empty. A train had just left.

I could have taken the next one and hidden outside Teiji's apartment to see if they were there. I didn't. If they had gone to his place, they would be there all night. It would be my final option. In the meantime, I headed back to the barriers for the shinkansen tracks, the place where Lily and I had said goodbye to Teiji.

I approached cautiously. With my wild, wiry hair and tree-trunk body I am easy to spot from a distance. I stood beside a newspaper kiosk and peered around. Immediately a customer stood in front of me and obscured my view. The woman inside the kiosk was regarding me with interest. I bought a copy of the *Daily Asahi* and walked quickly to a pillar.

I was both satisfied and appalled. I had been

right. Teiji and Lily were standing together, as lovers. They were face to face, Lily's left foot between Teiji's feet, their thighs almost touching. Teiji whispered something into Lily's mouth and they kissed. I wanted to escape quickly and silently but another, uncontrollable part of me wanted to do something quite different. I let out a loud cry, the lonely howl of a wolf to the moon, and was horrified to see Lily and Teiji turn and face me, wide-eyed.

I dropped my newspaper and ran.

Twelve

Kameyama and Oguchi have forgotten me. I lift myself to my feet, walk around the room. My joints ache. I clear my throat a few times, hoping someone outside will hear and remember that I'm still shut away in here. My restlessness is due to a sense that perhaps my story of Lily and Teiji has reached its end. Of course, it hasn't. I would be fooling myself if I allowed the thought to persist. The worst is still to come.

I called Natsuko the next morning and told her I would not be at work for several days. I'd been working on a translation for a steel corporation – instructions for the maintenance of a blast furnace – and the deadline was near. Though it went against my professional pride, someone else would have to do it. Natsuko was surprised.

'Lucy, what's happened? Are you ill? You've

never missed a day of work.' She thought for a moment. 'I bet you never even missed a day of school.'

That's true. I never missed a single day, not even for Noah's funeral. 'I can't come to work this week. It's impossible.'

There was a pause. She knew me well enough not to ask questions that probed areas of pain.

'OK. Do you need anything?'

Yes, I needed many things but I didn't know what to call them, how to ask.

'No, I don't. Thank you.'

I shut the curtains and locked the door. I lay on my back on the wooden floorboards, closed my eyes.

All day long, cars came and went in the garage forecourt. The attendants shouted as they waved customers' cars into position by the pumps. I listened to the endless humming of engines punctuated with human voices.

And I stayed in that position, more or less, for three days. I made occasional trips to the kitchen or bathroom, but mostly I lay on the floor, listened to the garage. Sometimes my fridge seemed noisier than the cars and vans, sometimes I didn't hear it.

I'm not sure whether I slept at all during those days and nights, or whether I lay there awake. It wasn't despair that kept me on the floor, or bitterness. All I felt was nothing. A complete and perfect emptiness. I had been in possession of a lover and a friend. Now I had neither. They had stolen themselves and each other from me. There was nothing to be done and so I did nothing. I can't believe, when I cast a glance of hindsight from the police station to my apartment during those three days, that I intended to lie there for ever, until unconsciousness or death. I suppose I was waiting for something but I don't know what it was. I had no intention of speaking to Lily or Teiji again.

On the fourth day, the phone rang. I let it go on all morning. I knew it was Lily – no one would try my number so often if they were at work – but I couldn't bring myself to unplug the phone. I wanted to know she was trying to speak to me, even if I refused to let her succeed. In the evening I walked out of the house toward the station. I didn't have any destination or route in mind but I couldn't stay in the flat with the telephone whining at me like Lily's voice.

I walked and walked all night. From Gotanda I set off toward the next station on the Yamanote line, going anti-clockwise. The road to Osaki was quieter and darker, all houses and no neon. I was glad to be outside and let the fresh air tingle against my stiff body. But when I stopped walking in Osaki, I thought of Lily and Teiji again, the handkerchief and ice cream that changed hands, their desertion of Lucy on the cliffs. I continued to walk because while I was moving my thoughts moved faster, and were less clear, less able to cause fresh wounds. I found myself following the train tracks to the next station and then the next.

Arrival at each station was a kind of homecoming for Lucy that night because she knew them so well, had lived different zones of her life in these parts of the city. There are twenty-eight stations in the ring around Tokyo, twenty-eight beads in the necklace. To me, each one has always been a unique gem. At Shinbashi I passed the old steam engine where I'd once waited for Natsuko before we caught another train to Odaiba. There we rotated in a little capsule on the huge Ferris wheel, looked out at Rainbow Bridge and Tokyo Tower, industrial plants and the grey sea. At Yurakucho station I ran my fingers along the sooty bricks of the railway arches. Under these broad curves are small restaurants. Bob and I sometimes met in one for dinner. He would ask my advice on every aspect of his life. I think, because my Japanese was fluent, he credited me with knowledge and understanding I didn't have, but I always did my best. Over spicy Chinese food he told me of his plan to become a rock star although, at forty-one, he knew it was getting late. He confessed that the dental treatment that brought our paths together had included cosmetic work with this aim. I'd never heard him sing so I had no advice that day.

Tokyo station came and went quickly. Many train lines converged here, undistinguishable, a row of nameless soldiers lying flat in a box. I couldn't guess which was the Yamanote, but when the lines separated again, I followed my feeling and was right. The next set of lights and platforms belonged to Kanda.

By the time I had come to the ninth or tenth station it seemed pointless going back the same way. I paced on. Akihabara, Electric Town where Teiji and I had looked at cameras, though he never bought any, strangely calm at night. Ameyoko where I went shopping with Natsuko to buy cheap food from the sprawling street market. It was quiet but I could almost hear the daytime voices of the gruff men shouting about their wares: slippery squid, fish, tea, coffee, shoes. Under the railway arches, yakitori bars, now closed. At Ueno the park where I'd gone to view the cherry blossoms in my first year, not realizing that it would be so packed with revellers I would hardly see the treetops. Yanaka, the cemetery where I'd sat before I went to Mrs Yamamoto's house. It rose uphill from the train tracks and beyond. At night the tombstones looked like silhouettes of people, sitting there on the hill, whispering secrets in the dark. Then, garish pink love hotels advertising rates for a night, cheaper rates for a 'daytime rest'. I went over the top of the loop, round to Ikebukuro, past a dark old shrine at Komagome and toward Teiji's terri-tory. If I'd ever looked at this on a map I would have noticed that Takadanobaba and Shin-Okubo lie in the north-west of Tokyo, but there is no reason why that should surprise me now.

Hours passed. Though I was already miles from home, my landscape didn't change so much, only the features in the foreground: nightclubs, love hotels, tombstones, parks, markets, shops, em-bassies. These were all contained inside an end-less corridor of anonymous rectangular buildings and railway tracks. I looked up at windows. Most were dark, showing just the dull outlines of curtains and blinds. Here and there bright squares of yellow glowed like feline eyes. Occasionally a figure moved inside. I looked to try and see the person, get an impression of their age or clothing, their movements within the room. Each time, I wondered who the person was. Of all the millions of people who worked, woke, slept in this city, stacked up individually and in groups, inside little boxes of home and work, which one was I spying on? I wanted to know these strangers who moved from one box to the next, transporting themselves around the city on such vast structures of rail and road. I wanted to know them because I was one, too.

Sometimes I lost sight of the Yamanote tracks and had to make my way around shadowy side streets until I found them again. Bright vending machines displaying drinks and cigarettes provided light in dark alleys and corners. At other times I was able to walk for a few miles without losing sight of the railway. On I marched, and in the early hours of the morning found myself in Shinjuku, metres from the spot where I'd first seen Teiji. I thought of Sachi. The small theatre where Teiji found her could be a street or block away from me, for all I knew. I wondered how much time had passed between Sachi walking out and Lucy walking in. I'd imagined her to be buried in the deep past, the way her photographs were buried in the box, but perhaps Teiji had moved from Sachi to me without stopping and then from me to Lily, as though we were three stations along a track.

I walked down the road that passes by Yoyogi park. I couldn't see inside but the treetops stood tall and feathery above the walls. I heard the song again that we sang that night. '*Ue o Muite Arukou*.' I cried but didn't bother to lift my head to stop the tears falling out – as the song instructs – because there was no one around and I might as well let them fall as they wanted. I came to my office in Shibuya. I'd never been there at night time and was pleased to see it. Perhaps it was the only place in Tokyo where I could feel at home now, without Teiji or Lily. I might return to work in a day or two. It would put my mind at rest to know that the blast furnace translation had been completed on time and to a satisfactory standard. As the sun grew bolder and people left their houses for work and school, I was walking from Ebisu to Meguro and finally I arrived where I'd started.

Gotanda. I had walked the distance of a marathon.
I had circled Tokyo.

The phone was still ringing as I entered my flat. I
ignored it and filled a bathtub of hot soapy water.
My feet were throbbing and burning. I sat in the
bath with water up to my neck and shut my eyes
to the sights of the clubs and bars, the graveyard,
the apartments and their washing lines, the railway
track endlessly criss-crossing other lines heading
all over Tokyo and Japan. And the carriages and
engines that slept at the sides of the tracks, tucked
away, empty.

My feet still hurt when I emerged from the bath.
They were pink and purple, swollen. I walked as
if I were trying on ice skates for the first time and
was hobbling from the changing room to the ice-
rink. The phone rang and rang. I picked up the
receiver, didn't speak but waited. Lily's shrill voice
was loud and clear.

'Lucy. Are you there? I've tried to ring you so
many times. Erm. I wanted to tell you that I'm
so sorry about what you saw. What happened with
Teiji – we never planned it.'

You accidentally arranged to meet him at the

station after I'd gone? I couldn't open my mouth to speak but the words screamed inside my head.

'And I feel awful. I don't know what I can say to you.'

So why did you call me?

'I know it must have broken your heart.'

My pulse quickened. My face and neck burned. What did Lily know about my heart? I inhaled two lungfuls of air so that I could say my next sentences without stopping for breath.

'My heart is a complex organ consisting of muscles, valves and blood. It can be weakened, it can have an attack and it can even stop altogether. But it can't break. So don't phone to tell me that you've decided my heart is broken.' My eyes were swimming in tears. I blinked to see better and hot water fell all over my cheeks. 'My heart is fine.' My voice cracked. 'But I can't move my feet.'

'Your feet? Lucy?'

I put the phone down and immediately the doorbell rang. Since I knew it couldn't be Lily, I blew my nose, wiped my eyes, crawled to the door and hauled myself up to unlock it.

Natsuko stood before me with an armful of yellow poppies. The petals brushed against the ends of her hair.

'Lucy, what's going on? Are you sick?'

'I'm not so well. I'll be fine in a day or two.'

'You look terrible. For God's sake go and see a doctor, find out what's wrong. Have you been crying?'

'I don't need to see a doctor. Anyway, I don't believe in them. It's tempting fate to see a doctor when there's nothing wrong with you.'

'In that case see your friend, Lily. Isn't she a nurse? Why don't you ask her to drop round?'

I stared at her.

'Lucy, what is it? What's happened?'

I wanted Natsuko to know, but I wanted her to know without my telling it because I couldn't bear to hear myself recount the story. I couldn't do telepathy so I shook my head.

'It's something to do with Lily. What's she done?'

'Leave me, please.'

'All right.' She sighed, kindly. Her voice sounded Irish today. I don't know which years or months of her life she spent in Ireland but this accent emerged only occasionally. 'I miss you at work. I'll call every day till I'm satisfied you're all right. Oh, I brought you these flowers. I saw them in the shop and thought they were such an incredible colour they'd have to make you feel better. I hope they work.'

I nodded. 'Thanks. Me too.'

She left and I was at a loss. I didn't want to sleep but I lacked the energy to walk again. The flowers were sunny and friendly. I decided to put them in water. I had no vase because I'd never thought of buying cut flowers for myself and I'd never been presented with a bouquet. I put them in a bucket. They didn't look good. I found an old plastic bottle and cut the top off, filled it with water. It was better than the bucket but the poppies didn't seem as beautiful as when Natsuko had held them. I took an old piece of black wrapping paper from my kitchen bin and glued it round the bottle. It made a perfect vase for the flowers but since all my curtains were closed – I hadn't opened them for four days – the room now seemed dingy. I opened the curtains, then the windows. Sunlight flooded in, the same colour as the poppies.

I rubbed cream into my feet until they were soothed. Then there was no stopping me. I went onto the balcony, loaded the washing machine with stale, dirty clothes and switched it on. I scoured away the tide mark in the bath, threw away the three empty toilet rolls that had been lying on the floor, damp and soggy, for weeks. I sprayed the mirror, wiped away dust and flecks of toothpaste till it sparkled. I wasn't ready to face my own reflection yet, but I was coming closer to that moment. In the kitchen I washed cups and plates, scraped grey scabby mould into the bin. On my hands and knees I swept away thick furry dust that lay behind bookshelves and in the corners of the room. I wiped the television remote control, button by button. I squirted and rubbed away a stain that had been on the television screen for months. I hadn't disturbed it before because it looked like Teiji's dried semen and therefore it was precious, though I couldn't see how it had got on the television. It was probably spilt food.

The washing machine beeped. I took my damp clothes and hung them on the line. I dragged my futons from their cupboard and flung them over the balcony railing to air. I bashed them with my pink plastic futon beater and watched the dust rise in little clouds then disappear. I vacuumed the whole apartment. Finally, when I could think of nothing else to do, I vacuumed the balcony.

I drank tea and listened to Dvořák. I went to the greengrocer's and bought shiny red apples to put on the table with my yellow poppies. Then I curled up on the floor and slept, a deeper, calmer sleep than I'd known for days.

And in the early evening a cool breeze entered through the balcony door, crossed my flat and went out of the window at the back. It woke me gently and I sat up. Slowly, not entirely awake, I went out and began to unpeg the washing.

The doorbell rang once more. I'd had Lily and Natsuko today, could this be Teiji? I guessed not. I already believed I wouldn't see him again. But I found myself wanting it to be Teiji. I had just unpegged a pair of tights and, rather than walk five paces along the balcony to my washing basket, or attempt to re-peg them, I put them over my shoulder. It was not a big deal, not a conscious decision. I just put them there while I went to answer the door.

Lily faced me in the doorway. She was shaking nervously. Her hand went up to her cheek and down again, several times. I fixed my eyes upon hers. She made her case; she hadn't wanted to hurt me, she just got caught up in the excitement of the weekend. If anything she'd done it to hurt Andy, not that he would ever know of course, but that might have been what was in the back of her mind, she thought. She wasn't sure if she and Teiji had a future together but if I wanted to be friends still, she would give up Teiji. She would go and tell him now that it was over.

'So is it OK? We're still friends?'

'No, we are not. Goodbye.'

And I closed the door.

I am confused about my feelings at that moment. I know that there was a part of me that felt sorry for her. She was a pathetic sight, standing on my doorstep quivering before me. I am sure that she was shocked by what she'd done and I also acknowledged that it was brave of her to come and face me. I know I had those feelings. But I know that I was also disgusted, and freshly angry. She would give up Teiji if we could be friends, but if not she wouldn't? Hearing her say Teiji's name sent me back to Tokyo station, to the moment I cried out, the way they turned to stare at me. My pity for her dissolved. I hated her, for stealing my lover and deserting me as a friend. I stood behind the door, wondering why I had let her off so lightly. My anger grew until I shouted out in rage. I don't know what words I bellowed to my four walls but after a few seconds I could hear my neighbour's vacuum cleaner above my voice.

I went down into the street to find her. It was only a couple of minutes after she'd gone, but she wasn't there. I thought I heard a quiet burst of laughter but I didn't see anything and the noise stopped as soon as it had started. I walked a little further along toward the station. My eyes were opened as wide as they would go and I used them like searchlights, beaming from one side of the road to the other, shining in every corner and nook. The muscles ached but I didn't want to blink or narrow my eyes for a second, not until I'd found her. I arrived at the station but she wasn't there. I turned back. It was odd. Even if she'd run to the station she couldn't have had time to get there, buy a ticket and get on the train. It was a long, straight road and I would have seen her ahead of me. A couple of cars sped past and then the world went quiet. I heard nothing but my footsteps on the pavement.

I won't deny it. I wanted to kill her. I wanted to wring her neck and kick her till she stopped moving. I wanted her to know how much pain I could cause in return for her betrayal. But I didn't

want to stab her. I didn't want to dismember and
decapitate her, throw the pieces into Tokyo Bay. It
never even went through my mind.

Thirteen

The officers are back. There is a new one. He is older, bigger, looks tough. His name badge says 'Suzuki' (bell tree).

'We are investigating the murder of a young, innocent woman.'

Not so innocent. 'I know, but I didn't do it. I could never have done that to Lily.'

'You know what's strange about you?'

I meet his stare. *Go ahead.*

'It's interesting. Normally when a corpse turns up, the friends and family of the victim are determined to believe that it cannot be the body of their loved one. Until formal identification takes place, they will not accept what may be obvious to everyone else. And sometimes even then they do not accept it. In your case, though, there seems to be an unstinting willingness to believe that the body found in Tokyo Bay belonged to your friend, Lily Bridges. Strange.'

I don't understand him.

'The body wasn't Lily's?'

'No, it was not. And yet you were so sure.'

He doesn't know my track record, the number of corpses scattered through my life, and that this next one seemed natural enough, inevitable even. I wasn't surprised when I read the newspapers. As soon as her boss had reported her missing, I knew Lily was dead. I don't mention this, though. It could be used in evidence against me. Found guilty. The accidental serial killer. The serial accidental killer.

'Then whose was it?'

'We don't know. It's not identifiable. The newspapers were a bit carried away when they made their assumption that it was Lily Bridges. Of course, it suited you to believe that. Anyone can see you could not have chopped up a whole body in a different part of Tokyo in so little time.'

'Besides that, I didn't even want to.'

'But you see, the body of your friend *was* found last night, in an unused shed behind the petrol station, just a couple of minutes from your home.'

I'm beginning to see his point.

'She was strangled.'

What is the stench around me? Is it the decaying flesh of the severed pieces found in the bay? Is it the smell of the shed, in the shadow of my own home, where Lily's cold body was encased? No, it is the smell of my own vomit.

The police are too professional to let my mishap loosen their glare. I raise my watery eyes apologetically but there is more to come. My friend – the glass of water friend – hands me a metal waste-paper bin just in time and snatches his arm away, though not fast enough to avoid a little splashing.

And I am empty.

Fourteen

'And that's not all.'

I'd hoped it was.

'We've learned of your relationship with Matsuda-san.'

'I don't know anyone called Matsuda.'

'Don't lie. Matsuda Teiji. Weird guy who works in a noodle place. His uncle says he's in Hokkaido now.'

Teiji's uncle. Soutaro. Lucy's only remaining link with Teiji. She frowned and considered his story, what she knew of it.

Soutaro was born in northern Tokyo and grew up there, just outside the Yamanote line. In his pre-war childhood this meant that he felt almost provincial. Now the city had sprawled so far that his address was positively metropolitan. He was proud to be from Tokyo. Osakans were too loud and Nagoyans were flashy and spent too much money. Tokyo was the heart of Japan.

During the war, Soutaro was evacuated to the mountains of Gunma and escaped the firebombing of Tokyo that swept away most of his family. His father and younger sister survived. He returned to Tokyo determined to be a part of its rebuilding. He and his father set to work and opened a small restaurant in the neighbourhood of Takadano-baba, serving noodles. Soutaro was proud to work there, serving to his fellow city-dwellers this most basic of dishes.

His sister married and moved to Kyushu. Nineteen years later – though it seemed to Soutaro like nineteen months – she returned. She brought with her a spindly son who looked as though he would never be good for a day's work.

Soutaro was proved wrong. This strange, brooding nephew, prone to sudden energetic bouts of laughter, worked hard and became strong. He seemed content mopping the floors, throwing out the old food, drawing up orders for ingredients. He worked all day and then in the evenings he wandered off, who knew where to. When Soutaro's sister died, there was no question but that her son should continue to work there. Soutaro had never married and liked the idea that upon his death the shop would belong to the son of his sister. But since then, the boy had become something of a worry. What was he doing with that camera every day? Why did he have no friends except for that sullen foreign girl? Soutaro was just ready to speak to Teiji, to suggest that it was about time he got married (and not to a foreigner), when strange things happened. Teiji went away for a weekend, to Sado Island. When he returned he seemed jumpy and nervous. A couple of weeks later, Teiji left a note on the counter of the shop, held down with a roll of undeveloped film. He was going north, to Hokkaido, to try his luck.

Soutaro couldn't continue without Teiji. His back was bad and he was ready to retire. He had the film developed, hoping that Teiji had left him a clue, but the pictures were strange shots of deserted beaches, railway tracks with no trains, boarded-up buildings, abandoned dustbins. Emptiness. He looked at them from every angle, turned them upside-down. He put on some old 3-D spectacles that had come with a wildlife magazine and peered at each photograph again. Finally he threw the pictures away and sold his shop to a stranger. In his apartment he sketched flowers and birds onto backgrounds of deserted places. He knew he wouldn't see Teiji again.

Matsuda Teiji. Teiji Matsuda. How had I never known his surname? I am shocked that in a country where family names are used over given names, I'd somehow evaded Teiji's. I must have seen it on an envelope, or something in his flat, or heard a regular customer asking for him by his name. But no, I hadn't. And now, more than when I'd seen him at the station with Lily, I feel I hardly knew him, that he has fooled me and eluded me.

'Yes, I knew him.'

'You were his girlfriend. And guess what. He left you for your friend, Lily Bridges. You were so upset that you didn't even go to work for over a week.'

Natsuko must have talked to them. Or even Bob. Lily may have sought his advice before paying her visit to Lucy. She may have told him what she'd done with Teiji. But there is no use in accusing friends. It is equally possible that my neighbour deduced, and gave them, this information.

I'm feeling dizzy, the way I felt on Sado Island before I collapsed on the clifftops. My hands reach up for my face. I rest my elbows on my knees, hold my chin in both hands. The room is hot. My jeans are stuck to my legs with sweat and sick. Someone gives me a bowl of cold water and a cloth. I rub the wet cloth on my arms and legs, twist it in the bowl, wring it to squeeze out brownish drops. I put the cloth in the bowl. It floats and bobs against the surface. I feel cleaner, cooler.

Now my mouth is moving, talking and talking though my tongue feels as if it's been anaesthetized and I sound drunk. I'm telling them what they want to hear. The story spills out quite easily, almost of its own accord. My insane jealousy of Lily is first, followed by the blind rage that threatened to consume me like fire when she let me down. Next, I detail my obsessive love for Teiji, love that stopped me believing that it was over, that he no longer wanted me. Finally, the pair of tights that proved such an opportune weapon, and how I caught Lily off-guard because she was still willing to believe that I would be her friend and so she even smiled at me. The conclusion: Lily's squawk of surprise, her short and feeble struggle. Her heavy, lifeless body, still warm as I dragged it to the hiding place. I tell them the long, uncomplicated story and, finally, they are pleased with me.

A man leads me down a corridor. It seems different from the one I saw several hours ago. The walls are dirty. The floor is slippery under my feet. There are no fluorescent lights here, just single lightbulbs hanging, at intervals, from the ceiling. I close my eyes but the bulbs still dazzle, one by one.

No, I didn't kill Lily. Lucy is innocent of murder and guilty only of spinning a story. But she is also very tired. So many people have slipped through my butter-fingers, like rounders balls on a summer playing field, that I no longer trust myself. It is pointless to fight my arrest, knowing that I could kill again. I would like some time out of the sun, a rest. And after all, how innocent am I? How not guilty? If I had let Lily speak to me on the phone, she wouldn't have been in my street that night. It was I who introduced Lily to Teiji and I who persuaded her not to return to Britain when she wanted to. The defendant must decide how to plead. And here is my plea. Not guilty, but not not guilty. Not entirely guilty but not entirely innocent.

The truth may out in the trial, but for now I'll be the murderer.

I realize I'm not wearing my own clothes but garments of soft cotton. I suppose someone told me to change, let me take a shower. I don't remember it. I feel as if I might have been asleep but I don't know how much time has passed, whether it was an hour or a night, whether it's now the same day or it's tomorrow.

A flat, male voice tells me that I'm being taken to a room where a visitor waits. I wonder who has come to see me.

Could it be Teiji? Teiji with a full name he never told me of. Teiji who abandoned me for my friend, why did you do that, Teiji? That's the only question I shall ask if, indeed, you are my visitor. And the answer I'm hoping for is an impossible one, you see, because it's an answer that allows us to forget Lily, to go back in time to where we were before I let her in. And I think I see you through the open door but already you're vanishing into nothing, the way your voice dissolved before when it was all I wanted to hear. I wish you wouldn't go. But there, you have and my heart sinks. No. What was Lucy thinking of? I know my visitor can't be Teiji for he is in Hokkaido. He has no reason to come here and the police will never find him in the city or the mountains. He's disappeared already into thin shadows.

So then it must be Miriam, who's tired of waiting for me by the sea and wants a real daughter to look after her and cook for her, not Felicity, and as I think of her I wonder how she could come to Tokyo when she can barely leave her house, her pain is so bad that she sits in the same chair all day, and it's impossible so I think that it might be Jonathan here instead, who used to be a policeman himself, and he's come to take me home. I'm blinking now, because my eyes are salty and I can almost hear the sea, and I can make out his shape through the open door ahead of me but then, how would I know it's Jonathan? I haven't seen him since he was fifteen, sixteen, seventeen at the most. But there he is, and Miriam behind him, looking so old and haggard now, staring at me with sad eyes, and I see the brothers: Luke, Nathan, Samuel, Simon, Matthew, smiling at Lucy but without a trace of cruelty and she sees them quite differently, not a jeering pack in Boy Scout uniforms but happy, healthy little boys with shining eyes. They're small, and sweet. I'm glad to see them but if they've come to take me back with them, I'll have to let them down, poor children. They can't speak Japanese, I'm sure they can't, and that is half my language now, it's more than half.

But they've faded into dots and gone. It isn't Jonathan or any of the brothers. It's Lizzie with her trombone, her greasy hair and illnesses. She's come to play music and she wants me to return with her to work for the BBC. Of course, I'll tell her that I can never do that because I haven't watched British television for more than ten years and I won't know how to do the job. And I haven't seen my cello since Mrs Yamamoto died and musical instruments are very expensive, as George and Miriam always said. Lizzie, I'm sorry to say that it will be impossible to play with you.

Lizzie's voice says it's not her, silly, it's Brian Church and he says, no it isn't. But I'm becoming confused and making mistakes. I must keep it clear in my head. I'm not dead yet. Noah, Brian, George, Mrs Yamamoto, Lily. They'll have to wait. I'm still alive. I *am*.

I stand in the doorway, force myself to get a grip because I know I haven't lost my mind, I'm sure I haven't lost it. I count to ten, five times, ten times, twenty times. I wait a little longer to be certain.

And then I'm ready. I force my brain to produce a logical thought. It does. My logical thought is that the visitor can only be Natsuko or Bob.

I enter the room. I can't feel my legs any more. It's as if I'm being wheeled along on castors. A person sits in front of the window, facing me. The sun is shining through and my eyes are not accustomed to natural light. I can't make out any features on the face but I'm sure I don't know this figure.

'Hello, Lucy. Do you remember me?'

I swear I don't. I squint. Is she speaking English or Japanese? I understand her words but I don't know which language they're from.

'You don't look well. We're going to get you out of this place and then you'll be fine.'

She giggles and I blink. It is Mrs Katoh, the viola player.

I suppose she has come to accuse me so I begin my flurried defence.

'I didn't mean to kill Mrs Yamamoto. I really didn't. It was an accident. I just put the cello in a different place and I don't know why, but I didn't know she'd fall over it. I'm sorry—'

'What are you talking about?' She laughs again, a glass tinkle. 'We all miss her terribly but you can't get away from the fact that Mrs Yamamoto was always a clumsy so-and-so. She said as much herself. I knew she'd have an accident one day. I was always telling her.'

'Was she clumsy?' I try to remember if this was true but I can't even picture Mrs Yamamoto's face.

'Yes, she was. But that's not why I'm here.' She looks into my eyes, speaks slowly. 'I wanted to see you. I've read a lot of nonsense in the papers. I hope you're taking no notice. I want you to know that I'm going to sort this out and you'll be free soon.'

'But I don't want to be free.'

'Why ever not?'

'I've got nowhere to be. I'm going round in circles in Tokyo.'

'Well, then, you must return home, to Britain.'

'There's nothing for me. All the people are ghosts. It's not a home, you see.'

'In that case you must come and stay at my house, here in Tokyo. There's certainly no point in going back to your lonely flat with that despicable neighbour and all those noisy cars.' She pauses. 'It must smell terribly of petrol, too.'

'All right.' I say it to keep her happy because I'm still hoping to be convicted of murder.

Mrs Katoh's hopes, not Lucy's, have been realized. A day has passed and I have learned that I am to be released with no charges. The case against me was circumstantial and the police were unable to find a single fingerprint or DNA sample on Lily's body. Moreover new evidence has come to light.

After details about me appeared in the national newspapers yesterday, the police received an envelope. It contained two photographs. The first showed Lily at a McDonald's near my home. Investigations reveal that it was taken on the night of the murder, two hours after she was seen at my front door. The cashier who recognized her in the picture recalled that she and her male Japanese friend had some kind of communication difficulty. Both seemed distressed. She left her cheeseburger untouched but drank her Coke.

Probably, she died later the same night. One thing is clear to the police. Lucy's venture into the evening with her tights over one shoulder had no connection with Lily's death. I was outside for only ten minutes or so. And my neighbour had reported that she didn't hear me go out again that night.

The second photograph was quite different. It was a picture of a woman squashed up within close brown walls, head lolling to one side as if she no longer had the power to hold it high, dark eyes empty, like two fat plums.

There were no fingerprints on either photograph. The police don't know that Teiji took the pictures, but I do. And the pictures don't prove that Teiji killed Lily. But they show that Lucy didn't.

Teiji. Why were you waiting for Lily in McDonald's and what did she say to you? That it was over because she wanted to be my friend? Perhaps then you realized your mistake – you'd lose both of us – and thought you could come back to Lucy, if only Lily wasn't there. Was that reason enough to kill Lily? I don't think so. Is first-degree murder just a habit of yours, like taking pictures? Or perhaps it's part of the same habit, something to photograph for your collection, something to keep. Now, more than before, I wonder what became of Sachi. It seems Lucy has finally met her match in killing. But then, the evidence is only circumstantial. I, of all people, should not be too hasty to judge.

Fifteen

I'm lying on the balcony at Mrs Katoh's house. Balconies in Japan are generally reserved for washing rather than people, but I like it here. I can see through the railings. There's a small park with bushes and trees. It has a play area for children with a slide and swings, but there are no children, no people at all. Beyond the park is the local railway station.

Mrs Katoh is in the kitchen cooking dinner. I can smell fish and ginger frying. We've invited Natsuko and Bob for dinner and they'll be here soon. A long time has passed since I saw either of them but they were happy and friendly when we talked on the phone. Bob told me he's been recording songs and performing in clubs around Tokyo. His musical career is going well. Natsuko took over my most important translations and all our clients are happy. I can return to work when

I am ready. Bob and Natsuko know I'm innocent. There's no need for explanations or apologies. We're friends and to eat and drink together is enough for today.

I'm writing to Jonathan. It started as a postcard but has turned into a letter. I discover that there are things to tell him. I write about my job, then about Natsuko's camellia tree because I know he'll understand how beautiful it was, and I tell him a funny story of how I was wrongly arrested on a charge of murder. If I get a nice reply, I may even go and see him in Yorkshire at Christmas, for a few days. Lily's parents live only fifteen miles away. I expect they'd like a visit from someone who knew her in Japan. Then I'll return to Tokyo, to Mrs Katoh, because her house is big enough for two, she says. And she doesn't say, but I know, that she likes to look after me, to make a fuss and cook for me, to run the bath to just the right temperature each night and put out a clean towel.

I drop my pencil and turn my eyes to the station. It's good to watch people board the trains, a full platform become an empty one within a few seconds. The train carries them away. Another crowd floods through the barriers and the platform is full again, of what look like the same clothes, bodies, and faces. I like to listen to the announcements, the touching caution that to rush onto trains is dangerous, that we must be careful to stand behind the yellow line because an approaching train is also dangerous.

We had a neighbourhood earthquake drill the other morning. It was calm and orderly, deemed successful by the municipal authorities. Of course, you never know when the big one will strike, but there are a few small things you can do to increase your chances of survival. I'm still nervous of tremors but less so than before. And that is another reason why I like to be close to the station. The trains rattle past our street and shake the buildings with such vigour that it's easy to miss the other movements, the ones that start under the earth's crust.

Mrs Katoh calls me to say that Natsuko and Bob have arrived. Their voices chatter in the hall. I stand and stretch my legs. A train leaves the platform, zooms away past the houses and apartment blocks. The balcony shakes and I rest my hand on the railing. There's a noise somewhere in the sky that I can't identify but it reminds me of my old apartment and before I have a chance to listen carefully to tell if it is the earthquake bird, another train rattles loudly to the station. I shiver, pointing out to myself that the earthquake bird came only at night so this must be something different. But the sound carries with it a picture of Lily crouching under my table in the light of the street lamp, and another of her hunched-up body in the shed. I remember the woman, scattered in pieces deep in the bay, whose name I shall never know. And Sachi. The noise, or perhaps just an echo of it, is still in my ears. I look at the sky which has turned grey and heavy but there are no birds.

There is a moment of quiet. Then, a rustling in the trees as if someone is creeping toward the house. My skin turns cold. I am absolutely still. I tell myself it's the neighbours' dog but I know that dogs don't creep. My mouth is dry. And then I hear it. The unmistakable sound of a camera clicking. The whirr that follows it as the film winds on for the next shot. I look around for Teiji but see only trees and bushes. I listen for his footsteps but now the clicking seems to be echoing quietly around the park, in every direction, and I don't know which way to turn. I put out my hand and feel the rain, small hard drops of water landing one by one on my skin and on the leaves and the balcony railing. *Potsu potsu* it falls, then becomes heavier, like beads of ice. I turn to enter the house, but I know Teiji's waiting out here for me and I hope that the warmth of the home and of my close friends will be enough to keep me safely indoors. I hope with all my heart it will, and yet—

It is going to be difficult.

Visit **www.picador.com** to read more about all our books and to buy them. You will also find features, author interviews and news of any author events, and you can sign up for e-newsletters so that you're always first to hear about our new releases.